TREASURE HUNT 2000

J. M. Wilson
Cathy Zolkowski

Verona Publishing • Edina, Minnesota

TREASURE HUNT 2000

Copyright © 1999 by J.M. Wilson. All rights reserved.

Library of Congress Catalog Card Number: 99-96836

ISBN 0-9667037-2-3

If you purchased this book without a cover, you should be aware that this book is stolen property. It was reported as "unsold and destroyed" to the publisher and neither the author nor the publisher has received any payment for this "stripped book."

This is a work of fiction. All characters, incidents, and dialogues are products of the author's imagination and should not be construed as real. Any resemblance to actual events or persons, living or dead, is entirely coincidental

Published by Verona Publishing, 3300 Edinborough Way, Suite 209, Edina, Minnesota 55435

No part of this book may be reproduced or transmitted in any form or by any means, electronic or mechanical, including but not limited to photocopying, recording or by any information storage and retrieval system, without permission in writing from the Publisher.

First Verona Edition, 2000

Cover Illustration & Design: Janie Sorheim

Printed in Canada

Contents

Chapter 1 1

Chapter 2 13

Chapter 3 23

Chapter 4 33

Chapter 5 49

Chapter 6 59

Chapter 7 71

Chapter 8 81

Chapter 9 91

Chapter 10 101

VIII

Treasure Hunt 2000

Chapter 1

It was a cold morning. Winter had unfortunately come in full force. Outside, large lacy snowflakes sparkled in the sky, parachuting ever so gently to the ground. It was the first big snowfall of the year. The old dull colors of the past were replaced, if but for a moment, with vibrant white. A gray Honda Prelude cut deep grooves into the snow. In the back seat two girls, one with shoulder length, straight, black hair and the other with slightly longer strawberry blond hair, bounced up and down as the car followed the rises and dips of the highway. Marci, the slightly shorter girl with the black hair, felt as if she were on a trampoline, bouncing up and down at gymnastics practice. Marci was having fun. She turned around to look out the back window and watched a wispy cloud of snow swirling in the vehicle's wake. After

Treasure Hunt 2000

traveling for fifteen minutes, the car gently turned to the left and gradually ascended a slight incline. Slowly the White, Rhode Island's largest international airport, rose .o view. The airport was located in the city of Warwick, out 20 miles from Marci's hometown of East Gree wich. Warwick, the state's second largest city, boasted 38 niles of beautiful coastline, with numerous salt and fresh water beaches. As such Warwick was a popular place f r tourist to visit. To accommodate the heavy traffic a new airport was built with building designs on the cutting edge of today's architecture. Its towering futuristic gray buildings were a welcome sight. To Marci the airport was a place of adventure and excitement. Its planes were but portals to carry her to new and unknown lands. One of the buildings, which her brother described as a plate glued on top of a stick, Marci imagined to be a flying saucer perched on the tip of a needle. It was an exciting time and Marci could hardly wait.

    She was on her way to visit her brother at a small private college almost a thousand miles away. Her brother, a college student in Minnesota had finally cut the apron strings. He had just completed the first semester of his freshman year. And from his letters, Marci knew he was enjoying himself immensely. His letters though short were inspiring. One such letter said: "Rat," that was his sister's nickname, "I'm having a great time. School is tough but fun. See you soon, Craig. A.K.A. "Mophead." Marci, having been to Minnesota once before when she helped her brother move his "junk" into the "dorm," had a pretty good idea of what to expect. The campus was lovely and the people were some of the friendliest she had ever met. Since starting college her brother had developed quite a penchant for blues music and coffee. Coffee shops were then certain to be some of the places to which he would introduce her. Craig had become such a connoisseur of coffee he even referred to it in one of his letters. "Rat, you won't believe what I'm doing at this very moment. I'm sitting in an abandoned jail that was converted into a coffee shop. To top it off, I'm also listening to blues music and sipping a mug of hot black liquid with mounds of whipped cream and caramel floating on top. I wouldn't have guessed it but this coffee stuff is really quite tasty, that is, if you make it properly. You should try it. Just remember… the more whipped cream, the better. Craig."

Inga, the other passenger, was Marci's cousin from Germany. As an exchange student she was only visiting for

Treasure Hunt 2000

a semester. Unlike Marci, Inga had never been to Minnesota before and was rather concerned about all the negative things Marci had told her about it. Of course Marci was only joking. Marci joked with Inga just like she did with her own brother. Craig knew her type of humor only to well. But Inga was unaware of the joke. Whenever Inga would ask Marci about Minnesota, Marci would always jokingly describe the state as "a very cold place filled with mean people that talked funny." Occasionally she would even mimic stereotypical Minnesotan speech patterns by elongating her vowel sounds. "Try to pretend like you're from Minnesota, they will be friendlier to you," she'd say. Marci's advice didn't help her feel any better. And to make things worse, they were traveling by themselves.

Since Marci's father wanted to make sure the girls would be safe, he had made all the necessary preparations for the trip. All the bases were covered. He arranged it so that at no time would the children be entirely by themselves. The airline was warned of the children's arrival and had made special provisions. A taxi was even commissioned, once the plane landed, to carry the children from the airport to the older and watchful eye of Craig; Marci's seventeen-

Treasure Hunt 2000

year-old brother.

Continuing on, the car turned and wove its way across a cushion of snow until it finally reached the airport. With a break and a skid the automobile slid to a halt. Since the children only intended to visit Craig for about a week they didn't have much to carry. Each girl carried one large suitcase filled with only the necessities. There were carefully chosen clothes to blend in with the college fashion and platform tennis shoes to look taller. Also there were numerous different colors of nail polish to give the finishing touch. Although the mass of nail polish took up a lot of room, Marci was also able to squeeze into her case another very important thing: Two walkie-talkies. She had purchased the walkie talkies about six months ago at a garage sale, and thought her trip with Inga would make a perfect opportunity to use them.

After they had finished checking in their luggage, all three headed to gate thirty-one. The children's gate lay somewhere in the middle of a long hall. They, along with numerous others, began their journey at gate number one. The numbers of the gates progressed in sequence. After gate number one came number two. And after gate number two came gate

Treasure Hunt 2000

number three. Like a long army of ants, the people all marched in step. As they passed by gate after gate, the crowd rapidly dwindled in size.

Apparently the gates that represented the most popular destinations were housed between gate one and gate ten. The hall had gray tile floors and white walls with large windows along one side. The decor was generic. The walk seemed to the children like an endless journey. It was a boring walk and Marci, an adventurous girl, couldn't take much more of it. She had to do something to make it fun and she knew just what to do. Treating the long hall like a floor exercise mat, she began jogging. As her speed increased and the hall emptied, she flew into a front handspring step-out round-off back handspring. Marci knew she was still in great condition because it had only been two days since her last gymnastics practice. It was not a difficult skill for her so she performed it flawlessly. Gracefully rotating in the air and remembering to arch her back the skill was conducted with elegance and beauty. Her father and cousin had seen her perform these skills many times before in some of the most unexpected places, such as: inside shopping malls, on the sidewalk, even in restaurants. So they were not too concerned that she would get hurt. Even so, her father cautioned her against doing anymore. "OK. dad," said Marci. "I'll stop." When she finished the series Marci turned and saw a girl about twelve years old who was staring at her in what can only be described as wide-eyed amazement. In her hand the little girl clutched a huge teddy bear. Around the bears neck hung a clanging array of bronze, silver and gold medals. When she saw the medals, Marci knew instantly that this girl was also a gymnast. A few years ago it became a popular tradition among gymnast to carry all their gymnastics medals around the neck of some kind of stuffed animal, usually a bear. The more the medals the better the gymnast. After a momentary pause Marci decided to break the ice. "Hi, um… are you a gymnast?" "Yeah," said the girl with an air or pride, as if the question was an insult. Marci could predict by the tone of the girl's voice that a competition of "who's the better gymnast" had begun. And if she wasn't careful their conversation would digress into comments like "I'm working on double fulls, how about you, what are you working on?" "Oh those I did those last year, now I'm working on triple fulls this year," "You are not," "Yes I am." "Then prove it, lets see you do one." Marci had been down this road many times before and had no desire to go down it again. Besides, Marci knew there wasn't any real competition because usually only younger gymnasts carried teddy bears. "So, what level are you?" asked Marci. "Level 6," said the girl proudly. "Oh that's good," said Marci. "With all of those medals I can see that you're really good." With her kind words, the competition ended. When Marci saw a big smile come to the younger girl's face she was glad that she had resisted the temptation to brag that she was a level 9. "Well I'd better get going, it was nice talking to you, and good luck this year," said Marci as she departed. "Thanks, you too!" said the fellow gymnast in a friendly tone.

Moving on, after a few more minutes of walking Marci and company came at last to gate thirty-one. At the gate Marci's father noticed for the first time that something appeared to be bothering Inga. Because they didn't have a chance to eat breakfast, he assumed it had something to due with hunger pains. As such, he checked his watch to see if they had time to get a quick snack before the flight. But there was no time. According to the schedule the passengers were due to board the plane in about fifteen minutes. The nearest concession stand was located too far away to make it back in time with out running. With food ruled out of the equation, he thought to lighten her mood with conversation. "You lucky girl," he said," you're going to have a wonderful time. Minnesota is beautiful this time of year. A slight smile formed on Inga's lips and her eyes sparkled a little. Those were the first encouraging words she had heard all week concerning Minnesota. Was it true? Was Minnesota a nice place? Inga glanced a discerning look in the direction of Marci, just in time to see her suppress a smile and look away. Marci's father continued, "and if you like shopping, Minnesota is a shoppers dream. They have one of the largest malls in the world over there... what's that mall called... ah... ah... I think it's called the American Mall," he said. Inga snickered and smiled, "I think ah...," she said pausing to formulate the exact words, "it's called the Mall of America," she corrected. Then she added inquisitively, "Is that located in Minnesota?" "Yes, of course!" her uncle stated emphatically. She gave another discerning look in the direction of her cousin. It was at that point that she realized that Marci had tricked her. Minnesota was great and not terrible like Marci described it.

Her uncle continued, "I hear the Mall of America is a great place! If you get a chance you should go check it out,

Treasure Hunt 2000

I'm sure it will be lots of fun." When Marci realized that Inga had discovered her little joke, she glanced up. The two girls' eyes met, each scanned the others face for a few seconds and then both broke out in laughter. Marci's father, not really understanding what was going on, just sat there and watched what he concluded to be an inside joke. "I'm sorry for letting the joke go on for so long," said Marci while catching her breath from all the laughter. "Minnesota is really a nice place, and its people are some of the friendliest in the whole world, even if they do talk a little different. Inga snickered, then tried to imitate a Minnesotan accent "Oh yeah... you betcha," she said jokingly. All three laughed in one accord. Marci's father noticed that Inga was in a much better mood. Her green eyes sparked with excitement behind a veil of red hair. Marci was also happy to see a smile return to Inga's face. Although she had not realized it before, this was the first time in days that Inga looked truly at peace and happy. "How odd," she thought, "that such a small thing like a joke can have so great an impact on people."

The time marched on. Before long, a voice was heard over the loud speaker, "Now boarding gate 31 for Minnesota." It was time. Before the children boarded the plane,

Treasure Hunt 2000

Marci's father brushed Inga's and Marci's hair aside and kissed them both. Have a nice trip," he said, "and, God bless!" The children did what any child would do and thanked him kindly while boarding the plane. When the plane finally took off from Rhode Island it did not take long to land without mishap in Minnesota. The flight was so short. Marci and Inga barely had time to even finish the complementary snacks, before the plane began its descent into the Mpls/St. Paul airport. The plane landed, and as expected they were met in the airport by an airline liaison, who directed the children to a waiting cab.

Treasure Hunt 2000

TREASURE HUNT 2000

Chapter 2

The children were directed to an old light-blue four-door sedan. It was built some time between the late eighties and early nineties. The car had passed through numerous hands, and had been involved in an untold number of minor traffic accidents. A large searchlight located by the driver's side mirror denoted its previous commission as a police cruiser. The car, parked under a stone awning, was shielded from the elements of winter, and shrouded in shadow. And as a result, the vehicle looked in relatively good shape from a distance. However, as the children approached, the car's defects became obvious. On one side of the car the children saw large areas of rust leaching through the blue paint. There were also at least a dozen small dents scattered along the side panels. The dents remnants of a hailstorm

Treasure Hunt 2000

made the car look old and dilapidated. Inside the driver who waited for the children looked totally bored. He was an older man somewhere in his forties, with hair, or what there was left of it, circling his head like a bushy brown crown streaked with gray. He was a large man at six feet one inch and two hundred sixty pounds. He had an unshaven face and large meaty hand.

When the children approached close enough to get a good look at the driver, his rough appearance and enormous size surprised them. Add that to the apparent wretched state of his vehicle and the children were more than a little apprehensive. The girls stopped in their tracks and looked at one another. Their thoughts were unspoken, each girl merely turn to see the reactions of the other in regards to the driver. Observing a mutual hesitation both turned simultaneously to look behind them at the airline liaison that had directed them to the rusty taxi. The liaison, who walked behind the children about twenty feet, was a woman of about thirty-five. She wore a standard flight attendant's uniform; a blue skirt, a white blouse, a red silky bow tie; all cover with a waist high blue sports coat. Because she didn't wear an over coat, she was reluctant to follow the children out side, but did so as a matter of routine. It was about twenty degrees Fahrenheit and the wind was blowing hard. In an attempt to stay warm, the woman held her arms folded tightly against her body. Her primary thought was to get the children into the cab as quickly as possible. With that done, her responsibilities would be complete. Then unencumbered, she would be free to return to the comfort and warmth of her office. However, her thoughts of a quick return to her office were interrupted when the children turned to look in her direction. In their eyes she could see that the children were more than just a little concerned. To keep things moving forward, she reacted quickly to encourage them. Forcing a smile, she nodded her head in affirmation. As she did, a gust of wind blew cold air against her teeth, chilling her to the bone. "It's alright," she said, "he's our best driver." With the acknowledgment that there was no mistake, the children continued on. At the cab Marci grabbed a hold of the back door handle and pulled it open. Partially because of the wind, opening the door was tough work. The door opened with a high-pitched squeak. Inga climbed in first while Marci held the door open. Then the liaison came and held the door for Marci. When all had entered the older women waved a quick good bye closed the door with a thud, then hurried back inside to warm herself.

Inside the taxi the children sat on seats cover with vinyl. The vinyl, cracked and torn, appeared in desperate need of replacement. The car also had a pungent smell of old cigarettes, which both girls found detestable. Despite their "gross" surroundings, the children force themselves to settle in and buckle their seat belts. When this was done the driver stared the engine. With a few sputters the engine took hold. "How ya' doin' back there?" asked the driver in a gruff and scratchy voice. "Do ya' want some heat?" Without waiting for the children's reply, he put the heat to its highest setting. Streams of Hot air began circulating inside the cab, defrosting the windows and warming the children. After about five minutes with the heat at its max, the girls began getting hot. "Is he trying to cook us?" joked, Inga in a whisper. Marci added to the joke, "No look," she said pointing to a half of a cheeseburger sitting on the front passenger seat, "he's already eaten." After a few chuckles the young women unbuckled their seat belts and took their winter jackets off. As they pulled at the jackets, the imitation leather seats rustled and squeaked. "Don't worry," said the driver mistakenly believing that the young women were getting impatient. "We'll be on our way in no time. I'm just waiting for them," he said motioning in the direction of the airport, "...to bring me your luggage." Moments later, a young man arrived with the children's bags. Once the luggage was loaded into the trunk, the driver began to leave the station. Carefully pulling away from the curb the car plowed through large ridges of brown slushy snow.

Unimpeded by the large building at the airport, as they traveled, occasionally, strong gales of wind would rock the car from side to side. After a rather violent series of gusts, Marci excitedly turned to Inga and whispered. "Driving in Minnesota is just like sailing on a boat." With bright eyes of excitement mixed with fear Inga nodded her head then turned to look out the frosted side windows. A heavy blank of snow poured from the sky like salt from a bad salt shaker. It was the heaviest snowfall of the year. Inga, unaccustomed to such extremes, watched the storm in amazement. The driver, an old hand at driving cab while Minnesota winter storms raged around him seemed unmoved by the blizzard conditions. Tooling along at a little under 50 miles per hour, his was the fastest car on the freeway. Some drivers had ei-

TREASURE HUNT 2000

ther exceeded their capabilities, fishtailed, then slid into a ditch. Most people were forced to reduce their speed to somewhere between 20 and 30 m.p.h. to facilitate a greater allowance for reaction time.

The road of choice was interstate 35W. From there they traveled to interstate 94 heading east. On I-94 a series of successive gust of wind struck the side of the cab. Jostled and pounded by the wind, the car shook violently. Inside, the children nervously gripped the vinyl seats in front of them and held on tightly. With a quick turn to the left, a little gas and then a quick turn to the right, the driver worked diligently to bring the car back under control. Although he labored diligently, all his efforts to prevent the car from spinning out were in vain. Like a pendulum, the back of the car swung to the right and to the left. Then as if in slow motion, the car whirled around 360 degrees. It seemed, to the girls like they were spinning for along time, but in actuality, they had made only one complete circle. The vehicle finally came to a gradual stop, partially blocking two lanes of traffic. Fortunately for all involved, no cars were in the vicinity. Due to the storm, interstate 94 west was relatively empty.

The excitement was over. In the back seat Marci and Inga

stopped holding their breath and exhaled a sigh of relief. The driver wiped the sweat from his brow and let out a long deep chuckle that sounded similar to the mooing of a cow. "That was a close one," he said as he slowly straitened the car and cautiously continued driving forward. Through his rearview mirror he looked at his passengers seated in back. A little disheveled because of the swerving of the car, Inga ran her fingers gently through her hair and brushed it behind her ears. Marci slowly released the seat in front of her. Her grip, strengthened by years of gymnastics training on the uneven parallel bars, had un-expectantly tore a large gash into the seat. Just as Marci started to stuff the cotton back into the large rip, the driver interjected. "How are you' gals' doin' back there? I hope I didn't scare you." He said in a deep voice. Although he had indeed scared them, Marci and Inga were unwilling to admit to it. "We're alright," said Inga reaching over to help Marci stuff the cotton back into the front passenger seat. "But your seat isn't," Marci added in a tone mixed with both remorse and pride. While driving with his left hand the driver reached his right hand around behind the front passenger seat to feel the damage. Lightly brushing over the old and cracking vinyl, his hand located a

Treasure Hunt 2000

large gaping rip. The tear was about three inches in width and around seven inches in length. "That's a big hole he remarked while glancing at Marci through his mirror. "You must have quite a grip." Marci smiled then blushed a little, "just like a steel trap," she added. Sense beginning gymnastics at the age of six, Marci had always been proud of her hand strength. Even on her time off, when there was no access to a gym, she would squeeze tennis balls to keep her hands strong.

The driver realizing the damage to his seat was his fault didn't want Marci to feel responsible. So he said some consoling words, "ah, it's not so bad, I'll just put a little duct tape on it," said the cabby. Marci looked away from the prying eyes of the driver. Even thought she recognized that a patch job with duct tape would make the cab look even more shabby and run down, she added with a note of humor, "yeah, a little duck tape in the right places and this baby is as good as new!" The driver, unable to keep from laughing, broke into a deep and boisterous cackle. "That's a good one," he stammered. "I'll have to remember that one!"

The car continued its journey east on I 94. At Snelling, one of the most traveled streets in Minnesota, they exited the highway and turned right. After driving about one mile down snelling they reached their destination. Craig's temporary residence was located on the corner of Snelling and Grand Avenue.

Treasure Hunt 2000

Chapter 3

The Children put their coats back on and buttoned them tightly. "Wait right here," said the driver. "I'll carry your luggage to the front door." The girls, in no big hurry to leave the warmth of the cab, did as he beckoned. After a short while he returned and played the role of a gentleman by holding one of the back doors open for the girls to exit. As he did, day light poured into the cab giving him his first unobstructed view of his passengers. "There you go ladies," he said. "Will you be staying long?" "No not long," answered the girls. Recognizing the girls might need his services again he reached into his pocket and pulled out one of his business cards. "Here," he said. "If you need another ride while you're in town give me a call." The card, crumpled and dirty, looked like he had carried it in his pocket for a long time.

Treasure Hunt 2000

The girls looked at one another feeling glad that they had made it to Craig's apartment in one piece. Marci took his card, and with no intention of ever using it she stuffed it into her pocket. "Thanks," she said. Then, pulling their hoods on, the girls stepped into the cold Minnesota winter. High overhead, large snowflakes shimmered like diamonds as they fell to the earth. As they walked toward the apartment, a gust of wind forced them to stop and huddle together. They waited until the wind slowed, then continued their journey toward the apartment. Approaching closer, the girls heard a low howl, like that of a wolf. The sound was the result of the wind, as it blew against a second story apartment window left slightly ajar.

The resident of the apartment, a seventeen year old college student, was also startled by the howling. He was awakened from a sound sleep. Climbing from his bed he went to the window and raised the blinds. The sunlight revealed a small rectangular- shaped room about eight by ten feet. Into such a small space, the student had managed to squeeze in: a wooden dresser containing four drawers, a desk covered with schoolbooks and papers, and a bed topped with a jumbled mound of blankets and sheets. All three pieces of

Treasure Hunt 2000

furniture rested on a tan carpet that was sprinkled with both clean and dirty clothes. After opening the blinds, Craig looked out from his window at the campus across the street. It was quiet. The crowds of students that normally filled the campus were gone for the holidays. Only a small fraction of the student population remained on campus to assist professors on independent study projects. However, most students at "Macalester" were less ambitious. The young man continued standing at the window looking out at his surroundings. A layer of freshly fallen snow made the streets look bright and clean. His apartment, located on the corner of Snelling and Grand, gave him a unique perspective on the college. Below he saw an eight-foot high, black iron gate surrounding an array of stone and brick buildings. Some of the buildings were quite old, such as the Old Maid, which was built during the 1880's. Others like George Draper Hall, which was Craig's dormitory when school was in secession, were built in 1997. His "dorm" had all the comforts of home: cable TV's, party rooms, and even athletic facilities. And besides all these wonderful things, "Macalester" ranked as one of the top twenty-four liberal arts colleges in the United States. Who could ask for more, Craig continued looking out

Treasure Hunt 2000

his window watching the snow fall. It was a beautiful sight. Looking high in the sky, he watched as large pieces of ice like meteors slowly came into view. As they approached closer, they seemed to gain speed. At eye level they appeared to rocket past his window and smash themselves into the earth. Craig was startled for a moment as he watched one of the larger pieces of ice smash against his windowpane. The window rung out a dull thud. Craig placed his hand on the window to feel the vibration, then chuckled in amazement. "Whew!" he exclaimed. "It didn't break".

From force of habit he then looked at his watch. It was Friday, the twenty-eighth of January, about twenty-five minutes after ten in the morning. The day was still young and school wouldn't start again until February the second. Craig's only obligation, for almost five days, was to watch movies, go to coffee shops, and drink loads of warm dark liquids while reading books or playing chess. At least, those were the only obligations he wanted to remember. After all, it was just too cold outside to do anything else. Craig rubbed his finger through his hair in an attempt to lay it flat and headed to the bathroom. When he finished brushing his teeth he washed his face with scoops of warm water and wet his hair so that it would be easier to comb. After combing his hair, he went to the living room and sat down on his favorite piece of furniture. It was a green futon his parents bought for him on his first day on campus.

Nearby, on the floor, he located yesterday's newspaper. He picked it up and glanced through page after page until he found the movie section. "Hmmm," he said aloud. "What do I want to watch." Within moments, he settled on an independent theater. The theater was playing a documentary on extreme sports. Not long after he had made up his mind, there came a loud knock at his door. The loud noise startled Craig. He rose to his feet to see who was there. Since he hadn't changed out of his pajamas yet, he opened the door just a crack and peered outside. Two figures stood in the hallway wearing similar styles of winter jackets except for color. One was navy blue and the other black. The long wool jackets fitted loosely, ended at the knees, and were fastened with overlapping wooden buttons. Each jacket had an unusually deep hood that the inhabitants still wore on their heads, enshrouding both faces in darkness. Craig spoke first, "may I..." Before he could finish his sentence, the figure wearing black forced his door open and barged into his

Treasure Hunt 2000

room. The other figure in blue accompanied. Craig knew only one person who would force his door open like that. His sister! She had arrived early! In truth, Craig had entirely forgotten that Marci and Inga were coming to visit. As such, he had made no preparations for their arrival.

"Rat, you guys are early," said Craig vaguely remembering something about them arriving supposedly at 12:30. Inga and Marci slowly pulled back their hoods and unbuttoned their coats. "Didn't you get our message," Marci asked. Craig glanced over at the telephone answering machine sitting on the kitchen counter. An iridescent green light flashed on and off, signifying that one message had not been heard. There was a moment of silence as Inga and Marci followed Craig's eyes to the flashing light. Inga smiled slightly, "you didn't listen to our message, did you Craig?" Craig walked over to the answering Machine and unplugged it. The green light stopped flashing. "What makes you think that?" he asked playfully. He then walked over to his apartment door, which still lay open. In the hall, he found two luggage cases. He carried the luggage into his apartment and set them out of the way of traffic against the wall. When he had finished moving things from here to there, his sister spoke. "Good," said Marci. "Since you knew we were coming so early and wouldn't have time for breakfast, what did you get for us to eat?" Craig thought for a moment about what to feed his guest, as a college student all he could offer was the bare necessities. "I don't know, what do you want?" he said. "Cornflakes or peanut butter on toast." "Do you have any juice?" asked Inga. "Sure, orange juice," came the reply. "Peanut butter on toast with orange juice," requested both girls. Craig took both of their jackets to his bedroom and laid them on his bed. In the privacy of his bedroom, he exchanged his comfortable cotton pajamas for a pair of jeans and a sweatshirt. He then went to the living room to set place settings for three. Because his apartment did not have a table, he set the place settings on the floor. The setting consisted of three cups and three plates. Then he headed to the kitchen to prepare the toast and juice. He returned within a few minutes with a plate of toast, a picture of juice, and a jar of chunky peanut butter. After taking their respective portions all three sat down to eat and drink.

Craig watched his sister and cousin as they ate. Judging by the large amounts of toast that they devoured, he concluded that they were quite hungry. When he saw that their

TREASURE HUNT 2000

stomachs were becoming content, he started a little small-talk. "So Inga, is your dad still enjoying being a college professor at St. John's University?" "Yeah, I think so," replied Inga. "What does he teach again?" asked Craig trying to keep the conversation rolling. "He teaches English," Inga quickly answered. While trying to think of something else to say, Craig noticed how different, the two cousins, Inga and Marci looked from each other. Inga had an oval face, green eyes, and long, sandy-blond hair with a tint of red. Then there was Marci, his sister, who had short black hair, dark brown eyes, and a pointy nose with freckles scattered about.

After keeping his company in silence for a few minutes, he finally came up with something else to say. "So, what do you guys want to do today?" Inga shrugged her shoulders, "I don't know, what do you normally do around here?" she asked. Craig saw at that moment, a prime opportunity to convince the girls to see the extreme sports film playing in uptown. "Well if you want to see a good movie, there's a really awesome skateboarding film playing. We could go see that," he said. Marci rolled her eyes at the suggestion, "yeah right," she said. "No way!" With the rejection of his first suggestion, Craig presented another. "Do you want to go to a coffee shop and listen to music? There's some really good bands around here." His suggestion of going to a coffee shop and listening to live music was favorable to all parties. The decision was made. Craig would introduce the girls to one of his favorite "hang outs," the "Jail Cafe."

Treasure Hunt 2000

TREASURE HUNT 2000

Chapter 4

Their plans were set. Marci and Inga would experience what Craig fondly referred to as, "the drink of drinks." "Which coffee shop are we going to? Is it nearby?" Marci asked. Craig ran his fingers through his hair as a slight smile formed on his lips. Watching Craig's boyish grin, Marci knew instinctively where he would take them. "Are we going to the coffee shop you mentioned in your letter? Are we going to the prison?" his sister asked with excitement. Craig's eyes brightened as he nodded his head in the affirmative. What Marci called a prison was in actuality a county jail. The distinction being, jails generally hold persons, some innocent and some guilty, for short duration's of time before trial. And prisons hold persons after sentencing for longer periods of time. Inga, who had been sitting quietly munching on pea-

Treasure Hunt 2000

nut buttered toast and swigging orange juice, looked up in surprise at her cousin's mention of a prison. "Is the cafe inside a prison," she asked hesitantly. "No ..." he said trying to set her mind at ease. "It's not in a prison! It use to be a prison thirty or forty years ago, but now it's a coffee shop!" "What happened to the prison?" Inga asked inquisitively. "It was too small so they had to build a bigger one a few miles away. But you really have to see this coffee shop. It's one of the funnest places in all of Minnesota," he said.

Then, knowing how much Inga enjoyed music, he added, "and they have some really cool bands." "They do? Like who?" asked Inga. Craig thought for a moment, "Well last week on Tuesday they had a group called Big Red Monkey ..." Craig paused for moment to see if either girl had heard of the band. Judging by their blank expressions, he assumed that neither had heard of them, so he continued. "Ah ... on Thursday there was a group called Three Rats and a Mouse." "Three Rats and a Mouse?" Marci chimed in "They're cool," she added giving a thumb-up. As expected, Inga had never heard of the band. Coming from Germany, she had little familiarity with local American bands, especially bands that played the coffee shop scene. As such, she

TREASURE HUNT 2000

followed Marci's lead and gave the band a thumb-up. The three friends continued eating and drinking. When they had finished, Craig collected the paper plates and cups and stuffed them into a large plastic bag to be thrown away later. His sister and cousin, pulling their luggage behind them, went into the bedroom to change.

It was a tough decision. Since neither had been to a coffee shop inside a jail before, what they should wear was a mystery. Judging from Craig's description, it sounded like a location where college students "hangout." So one thing was for certain, they didn't want to look too young. "They might get weird on us and ask us to leave," Marci feared and Inga agreed. The two rummaged through their respective bags looking for something to wear. The clothes were separated into two piles: those that made them look older, and those that made them look like kids. The distinction being, kids clothes were bright in color, baggy, or had a logo or symbol of some popular sportswear or brand name plastered somewhere on the front or back. The "older" clothes, in general, were more basic; earth toned and form fitting. It took roughly a half-hour for the girls to decide on what to wear. They must have each tried on at least 5 outfits. After

Treasure Hunt 2000

all the searching, Marci finally decided on a pair of well worn blue jeans with a woolen hunter green sweater. Inga chose a pair of jeans with a black cotton sweater. Since there was no mirror inside Craig's bedroom, the girls had to rely on each other. "How do I look?" asked Marci rising to her feet. To get the full picture Inga stood and backed up as far as Craig's little room would allow. Then standing with her back against the door, she slowly scanned Marci from head to toe. After a moment or two of standing and waiting, Marci began to feel uncomfortable. "Well?" she asked. "How do I look?" Inga could tell from Marci's tone, that she was feeling a little embarrassed. It was an emotion she had rarely seen her cousin exhibit. To her, Marci had always seemed confident about everything. The very thought that Marci could get embarrassed was comforting to Inga. It meant that her cousin was just like she was – a teenager who at times felt insecure. Inga smiled, "you look," she said with a pause for dramatic effect, "collegiate!" with a sigh of relief Marci smiled.

But now we need to do something with our hair," added Marci. Not wanting to settle for the usual ponytails, the girls attempted to do some of the more stylish 'hairdos' they had seen on TV. It proved easier said than done. After many trials and errors, Marci suggested one last thing. "How about braids?" "I don't think so," said Inga hesitantly. "Why not?" responded Marci. Not wanting to hurt Marci's feelings she added. "Because we'll look like a couple of girls from 'Little House on the Prairie.'" "Marci knew all to well what she meant. She remembered three years back when she visited Inga in Germany. Inga who was eleven at the time had two large braids sticking out, one on either side of her head. When Marci saw how she was treated, she encouraged her not to wear her hair like that. "It looks too much like a kid," she said. In order to calm Inga's fears she explained her idea. "Not the really big ones, I'm talking about French braids, you know the small ones that lie flat on your head. Or if you want, I could twirl your hair too!" Inga nodded her head that it was a good idea. Because she had seen people with their hair twirled before and liked the style, Inga opted for twirls. Marci opted for Braids. The twirling did not take long. Marci did Inga's hair in about fifteen minutes. The braids were more labor intensive. Because Inga had not practiced her braiding for almost 3 years, it took her about 30 minutes to do Marci's hair. After their hair was complete, only one more thing was needed to complete the en-

Treasure Hunt 2000

semble, shoes. Believing that height and age were correlated, Marci and Inga decided to wear their platform tennis shoes. The sole of each shoe made the girls look a full three inches taller. "That should do it," said Marci as she opened the bedroom door. "Now we look like college students."

Exiting the bedroom, the two girls joined Craig on the futon near the kitchen. In his hand, Craig held a bus schedule. Since he didn't have a car, a bus seemed the next best option for travel. "The next bus will come in about thirty minutes," said Craig. The bus stop was located on the corner, right outside his building, so there was little need to hurry. They waited for about twenty-five minutes, then headed downstairs to the bus stop. As planned, the bus collected the youths at the corner of Snelling and Grand at three in the afternoon. As they boarded the bus they noticed that it was pretty empty. Apparently, not too many people were around during the holidays. Of course, the girls wanted to go straight to the back of the bus, so they could talk as loud as they wanted without being overheard. They were so excited for their first day out on the town. The bus traveled down Grand and stopped frequently. On one of the scheduled bus stops, a friend of Craig's got on. Marci and Inga tried to keep a low profile so they wouldn't have to talk to him. "What's up Jason," said Craig. "Hey, Craig, what are ya doing out here? I thought you'd be glued to the TV. until school started again!" Before Craig could answer, he saw Marci give him a stern look. He knew that she didn't want him to blow their cover as "pseudo- college students." After some careful thought, he replied, "I just needed to run a few errands. I also need to get some food and I'm having coffee withdrawals, so I think I'll stop by the Jail Cafe". His friend looked outside at all the snow, then nodded his head, "that's the best idea yet," he said. Not too long after they traded some small talk, Jason signaled his intent to depart by ringing the bell. " Well, have a great week, Craig!" Thanks, I will, and you to," Craig answered. Craig was glad that the girls were sitting behind him. Otherwise he would have some explaining to do and in the process maybe ruin their disguise.

Travelling down Grand, they transferred to another bus, which took them right to their destination. The Jail Cafe, located on the corner of Exchange and St. Peter, was a square brick building with small windows. Many of the windows held old and rusting metal bars. The front door was made of

Treasure Hunt 2000

wood and glass. It had seen better days. As a result of its constant use, the door fit loosely in its hinges. Over the door, carved in stone, were the words "Ramsey County Jail." There were no bright lights to attract passersby and no large signs beckoning the masses to come. The cafe was like a landmark. People for miles around knew of its existence and where it was located by mere word of mouth. The three friends stepped off the bus. Then, chilled by the Minnesota winter, they hurried to the cafe.

The door opened with a loose wiggle. As it did, the teenagers were greeted with a rush of warm air that smelled of coffee and cigarettes. The light inside was dim and murky. The walls were black like coal. As they walked, the floor would crackle and squeak. The floor was made of old wooden planks. Over the years the planks had shifted, causing large gaps to form between the boards. These gaps then allowed puddles of muddy water to collect, due to patrons not wiping their feet carefully before entering. The dimensions of the room were about thirty by thirty feet. In the center was a long gray counter. Directly behind the counter rested the coffee paraphernalia along with two attendants. The attendants, one male and the other female, looked to be in their early twenties. Both wore earrings, black sweat shirts with the words, "Jail Cafe" emblazoned on the front, and blue jeans. Far in the background and deep in the darkness played a blues band. Its four male members, unshaven with stylishly ruffled and ragged clothing, played some of the most soulful and toe tapping music Marci and Inga had ever heard. Scattered about the room were numerous small circular tables. Green and made of metal, each table was encompassed by four brown wicker chairs. The shop was surprisingly crowded for the holiday times. Most of the tables had already been taken. The girls observed a couple near the front of the band preparing to leave. They hurried over to claim the empty table as their own. With the acquisition, the girls sat on the edge of their seats listening to and watching the band. To the left and right of the band were jail cells. The metal bars still remained, but the doors had long since been removed. Inside each jail were two tables with the usual compliment of chairs. Because proximity to the band was in high demand the two cells were considered the best seats in the house. The band, "The Blue Mountain Boys," who had played nonstop for an hour and a half, brought their current composition to a winding close. Then, setting their instru-

Treasure Hunt 2000

ments aside, took a short break to rest fingers and drink coffee.

No longer mesmerized by the music, the customers returned to speaking to one another. "How do you like the band?" asked Craig. Elated, both gave the band two thumbs-up. "Where's that great drink you were telling us about?" asked Marci. "It's on its way," said Craig rising to his feet and heading in the direction of the service counter. While the young women waited for their refreshments, they checked out the other people hanging out at some of the other tables. In one corner sat an older woman who looked to be somewhere in her seventies. Two tables behind her and near the wall Marci noticed a fellow with gray hair and dark circles around his eyes. Although there was no one at the table with him he was talking aloud to himself as if he had made some profound discovery. "Yes… yes… I've got it," he barked into the already noisy cafe. "I've got it." Because he quieted rather quickly, Marci didn't pay much attention to him. She figured he was probably excited over some stock transaction, and couldn't control himself. Besides, she was only looking around to see if Inga and she were dress appropriately. The man with the gray hair looked to be somewhere around forty five years of age. He was dressed in a long black coat and khaki pants. In one hand he held a newspaper and in the other held a mug of black coffee. On the other side of the room there was a group of fellow teens. Each wearing those cool looking lace chokers that looked, if worn properly like tattoos. "Well, at least we don't stand out," said Marci covertly pointing to both the oldest and youngest members of the audience. Inga relieved nodded in agreement, then slouched back into her chair and added, "now where's that drink?"

At the counter, Craig purchased three caramel mocha's, and a current daily paper. The paper he had at home was at least two days old. The drink looked more like some exotic dessert than a beverage. Each drink, covered with a swirling pyramid of whipped cream, was topped with a bright red cherry. Carefully holding the three drinks in his hands and the paper under his arm, Craig returned to his sister and cousin. When he had carefully given each girl a cup he took his seat. "There!" he said with a snicker. "Rat, and cousin of the Rat, I present to you the drink of drinks." Craig pulled the cherry off the top of his own drink and ate it. Then taking care not to burn himself, he raised his cup

Treasure Hunt 2000

and slurped some of the coffee. The whipped cream clung to his upper lip, forming what looked like a white mustache. Marci and Inga, neither particularly fond of coffee, watched his initial drink with anticipation. Was it all that he had said? Was it really that good? Then after noting a satiated expression of glee, the two girls ate their cherries and buried their mouths full into their respective mounds of whipped cream. "Your right," said Marci. "This is good." "Are you sure this is coffee?" inquired Inga. "It's like a dessert." "Yeah, isn't it great," said Craig. "It has all the advantages but none of the disadvantages." Craig raised his glass and took another long sip, then licked away the accompanying white mustache. Marci and Inga followed his lead, both drinking and licking.

The coffee shop was a success. Before long, the band began to play again, and the three friends sat in silence listening to music. While listening to the music Craig simultaneously thumbed through the local paper. As he did, an article on the front page caught Marci's attention. "Hey Mop, can I see that page?" she asked. Craig peeled the page in question off and slid it across the table to Marci. Marci read it. It was an article about a treasure hunt.

Treasure Hunt 2000

"Hear yea, hear yea, Come one come all, gentlemen, ladies and children too, the festival begins, we await for you.

On public ground the prize is set, the winner is still undiscovered yet.

In our seventy-fifth year, the reward is quite clear, with ten thousand, one can buy plenty of gear.

To find it one can search from on high then low, the discovery could be near, even under your toe.

That concludes our introduction, there is no more to say, save beauty is sweet but passes away."

It was an intriguing and mysterious article that sparked Marci's imagination. Marci folded the paper so that the treasure hunt article was front and center, then handed the paper to Inga. "What do you think?" she asked while tapping the paper with her index finger. Inga took the paper. Because of the dim surroundings she read the article with a squint. In an attempt to discover hidden meanings, Inga read the article twice, then smiled. "So what do you think?" asked Marci. "Do you want to do it?" "Yeah sure,"

Treasure Hunt 2000

said Inga as she nodded her head confidently. "I think we can solve it!" Marci and Inga informed Craig of their desire to participate in the treasure hunt. "That's a great idea," said Craig, relieved he no longer had to find something for them to do. "We can do the treasure hunt." At that the plan was set.

To do the preliminary research, Craig, Marci and Inga separated and asked some of the patrons that knew about the hunt, the fundamentals of the game. Such as, what was being searched for? And where was the search to take place? Minutes later they returned to their seats to compare notes. All discovered that they were not searching for money, as the children had originally supposed. But the hunt involved a small plastic semitransparent medallion about the size of a silver dollar. When the medallion was found it was to be turned in for a cash reward totaling ten thousand dollars. Further, the consensus was that the medallion was hidden in one of the parks in the city of St. Paul. Clues were to be given every day for seven days in the local paper. If at the end of the seven days the medallion was still not found, the money was to be turned over to a local charity. The work was divided as follows: Craig was to contact the park board and get in-depth maps of all the parks in St. Paul. He further was to highlight, streets, places, or things referred to in the daily clues. Marci and Inga chose the harder, and what they believed the more fun of the two jobs. It was their responsibility to go out and actively search for the medallion. The three teenagers were excited. No longer paying attention to the jazzy blues music that filled the background, the teens talked for a long time about the clues and what they meant. Though they talked and disagreed on many points, there was one point that they all held in common. All agreed that because the clue referred to searching, "both high and low," that the medallion was hidden in a park with a rather prominent hill. Perhaps the mound was even used for sliding or skiing. They continued their discussion well into the evening. When the band took another break, the teens collected their things and headed back to Craig's apartment. Inside, they ate a dinner of meatless spaghetti and prepared for bed. Inga and Marci shared the bedroom, while Craig, kicked out of his own bed, slept on the futon in the living room.

Treasure Hunt 2000

Treasure Hunt 2000

Chapter 5

Because Inga and Marci were eager to start the hunt, the night seemed to linger on forever. In the dark, both girls tried to block out all the excitement and force themselves to sleep. Although the girls tried to get a good night's sleep, the excitement was just too great. With their imaginations running wild, each was only able to sleep for a short duration. Too excited to try and force themselves to sleep any longer, the young women decided to "call it quits" and just stay awake. It was early. Outside their window, a full moon glowed in the night. The sun would not peak out over the horizon for another ninety minutes. After a short while of lying still, Marci slowly turned around to face Inga. Inga closed her eyes and pretended to be asleep, but the glow of the moon gave her secret away. Through the darkness Marci

TREASURE HUNT 2000

saw the soft yellowish light illuminating Inga's face. Inga's lips quivered a little, it was the type of nervous twitch that only happens when one is trying to keep from laughing. With the twitch as confirmation that she was awake, Marci pulled the covers up over Inga's face. "Have a nice sleep," Marci giggled, "this should help keep that bright moon from keeping you awake." With the realization that both were wide awake, the two girls broke out into loud laughter. "We have to keep it down," said Inga in a boisterous giggle. "It's too early, the neighbors are still sleeping." Both girls instinctively placed their hands over the other's mouth. Their uproarious laughter was quieted to a muffled snicker. Because it was so early, there was very little the girls could do that would not have disturbed the other residents. As a result the two cousins just lay in bed and talked. They spoke of hunting for the medallion and using the walkie-talkies to stay in constant communication. "It's better that we should split up and search. We can cover more ground," said Marci. "Yeah, It'll be like we're a couple of detectives on an important case," said Inga in a whispered voice. Liking the idea of being a detective, Marci added more to the story. "Yeah, we're like Sherlock Holmes trying to decipher the riddles of some evil genius, who's the greatest jewel thief that ever lived." Inga giggled, "Yeah we'll call it," Inga paused and both girls said at the same time, "the Mystery of the Lost Medallion!"

As the two talked on and on about all the fun they would have, the sun slowly but surely peeked over the horizon. The morning had finally arrived. After climbing out of bed, the two cousins began to dress for the hunt. Because they expected to be outside for long periods of time, they tried to dress as warmly as possible. Long-sleeve tee-shirts covered by oversized sweatshirts, were the order of the day. These were accompanied by jeans, two pair of socks and tennis shoes. However, they chose their regular tennis shoes instead of the platform ones this time. They needed to get around quickly and easily, and the extra inches on the platform shoes made running difficult. When they had dressed, they opened the bedroom door and stepped out. It was dark in the living room. Marci, feeling for the light switch, ran her hand down the side of one of the walls. Locating the switch, she flicked it on. A warm amber light filled the room. The futon that Craig had slept on was empty. Apparently Craig had gotten up even earlier than the young women.

Treasure Hunt 2000

Among the blankets and sheets that lay on top of the futon was a note from Craig.

> *"I've gone to get a map that has a list of all the parks in Saint Paul, and a paper: I'll be back soon. If you get hungry, there is a box of instant oatmeal on the counter."*

Craig had apparently visited the neighborhood store on the corner while his sister and cousin were still asleep. The store, small and expensive, was visited by college students only to pick up emergency items that they had forgotten to buy at the larger cheaper stores, or when the provisions had run out sooner than expected.

Since they couldn't start the search just yet, the girls could at least busy themselves with getting some breakfast. When the appropriate amount of water came to a boil, the two young women sat down and ate thick and sticky cinnamon-apple flavored bowls of oatmeal. Since she was not currently under the watchful eye of her mother, who would occasionally warn her to, "stop playing with her food." Marci took the opportunity to play with her food as much as she wished. She stuck a big clump of the oatmeal on to her chin.

Then she called to Inga, "How do I look," she giggled. Inga couldn't help but let out a boisterous laugh when she saw Marci wearing a beard of oatmeal that grew longer by the moment. "It looks good," said Inga. "But you need a mustache." Inga reached into her bowl and scooped up a glob of cereal on to her finger. Then taking aim she flicked the cereal at Marci. The glob hit Marci in the face. Marci retorted by launching a glob of her own, which found its way to Inga's hair. After that it didn't take long for a constant stream of oatmeal to fill the air. And before they knew it, oatmeal was everywhere! Because they were expecting Craig to come back at any moment and the place was on the verge of becoming really messy they decided to call a truce and clean up as fast as possible.

Craig returned before they had finished eating what was left of their breakfast. In his hand he carried a local map and a current paper. To keep from tracking snow into his apartment, he stomped his feet outside in the hall, then entered. "How you gal's doin'," he asked, as he plopped himself down on the futon. I see ya found the oatmeal." "Yeah we found it alright," said Marci trying to keep from cracking up as she scraped the last remnants of the thick cereal

Treasure Hunt 2000

from the bottom of her bowl. "It's really good, I hope it wasn't too much trouble," added Inga while letting out a couple of snorts of laughter with her mouth closed. Craig didn't understand what was so funny, so he just ignored it and answered her. "No, no problem at all. I got it from that store over there on the corner," replied Craig while pointing towards the window. Craig set the paper down in front of the two girls, then carefully unfolded the map. Inga and Marci opened the paper and eagerly read the second clue. After each had read the parable silently, Inga read the parable aloud.

> "Through endurance and patience a treasure is found. Within the ancient and the new, the victor might just be you."

"What do you think they're talking about?" asked Inga. Craig rubbed his hair. "I don't know," he mumbled to himself. "Maybe it's an old park going through renovations." Marci perked up then added, "or an old building being remodeled." It was a good start. With remodeling being the main focal point, Craig set to work and called all the parks in Saint Paul. He asked them if there was any new construction going on. Out of the 19 possible parks, only three were undergoing any substantial new construction, Sun Ray, Red Eye, and Conway. And of the three, Sun Ray, was the only park with a large and prominent hill. The hill was a popular place for skiing and sliding. Craig hung up the phone and circled the location of the park on the map. "This is the most likely place," he said passing the map to Inga. Inga looked at the map. The park was circled in red. Sun Ray, was one of the largest parks in the city. It had steep rolling hills and plenty of large trees, mostly elms, oaks and pines. Some of its amenities included a baseball field, two hockey rinks, and numerous out door tennis courts. From the map, the outline of the park looked like a toddler's attempt at drawing a rectangle, having uneven and jagged lines. The park was relatively close. It was located about two miles from the college.

"What do you think," asked Craig. "You girls wanna do this by yourselves or do you want me to go with ya?" Marci and Inga paused for a moment to weigh the pros and cons of his generous offer. On the plus side, three people searching could cover more ground than two in a shorter period of time; But on the negative side, Craig was older and thus would have a tendency to be bossy, especially if they were having fun. That being the case, from the perspec-

TREASURE HUNT 2000

tive of both young women, the negative outweighed the positive. The young women shook their heads. "Neh!" replied Marci. "We need you here. Don't worry, we'll do all the leg work." "You don't mind, do you Craig?" asked Inga. "Nope!" responded her older cousin. "Not at all." Given the alternative Craig couldn't have been happier. With the girls out of the way the extreme sports film was again a possibility. It was settled. The young women would actively search for the treasure by themselves. Craig called the bus company to find out which bus the girls needed to take, and its arrival and departure times. He wrote the information on a sheet of paper, so Inga and Marci wouldn't forget. With the travel information in hand, the young women headed to the bus stop.

Treasure Hunt 2000

Treasure Hunt 2000

Treasure Hunt 2000

Chapter 6

It was the middle of the afternoon, a late start for treasure hunting. The bus stopped at the corner of Conway and Ruth, at 2:30 PM. The ride to Sun Ray Park was uneventful. In comparison to yesterday, the weather was nice, about twenty-five degrees Fahrenheit. The sky was clear. The sun was bright. Like thousands of tiny diamonds scattered on top a bed of cotton, the sunlight made the hills and valleys of snow sparkle and glisten. Sun Ray was a large and beautiful park. Its mountainous terrain gave the children a sense of awe and wonder. Because of the nice weather, the park was full of activity. From what Inga and Marci could see, most of the activity centered around skiing or sledding. Nearby, Marci and Inga stood and watched the joyful crowds of parents with children laugh and play in the snow. Uncon-

Treasure Hunt 2000

cerned about the treasure hunt that was going on around them, they continued a carefree day of snowman construction, fort erection, and snowball fights. It was an exciting time. Both women were glad they had come.

After watching the children and their snowball fights, Marci took off her gloves and formed a snowball of her own. "Watch this," she said to Inga. "Do you think I can hit that tree over there?" Marci pointed to a baby oak. The tree stood about ten feet high, and its trunk was roughly forty inches in diameter. To Inga it looked like a long throw, about 100 feet, but because Marci was a natural athlete, Inga rightly figured it would be an easy task. "Of course you can," she responded, "that one's too close." Searching, Inga found a larger tree but much further away. "Why don't you try for that one?" Inga jokingly asked. Because gymnastics helped coordination, Marci was good at throwing things. Every year she took home a new stuffed animal that she won for her accuracy in throwing at the state fair. "OK," Marci said, "I'll go for that one." In moments the snowball was launched into the air. It was an amazing throw. The tightly packed snowball traveled in a straight line and was headed directly for the tree. It fell short of the destination by about ten feet.

TREASURE HUNT 2000

Both young women were surprised. Neither knew that she could throw that far. "That's a great throw," said Inga. "How did you do that?" "I don't know, I just threw it,"'" responded Marci. The young women continued throwing snowballs for a little longer to see if Marci could duplicate her first throw, but she could not.

After playing around a little longer the cousins decided it was time to search for the medallion. "It's probably somewhere near where they're doing the construction," said Inga. Then she questioned, "Is there an office where we can find out where the construction sights are?" "It should be around here somewhere," said Marci. Presently, both teenagers looked out across the park. It was a large park with lots of snow, trees and people, but as far as they could see no buildings. While they searched, an older man somewhere in his forties noticed them. A seasoned veteran of treasure hunts, the stranger wore an old green parka. His coat was speckled with dried paint and had patches on the elbows, denoting its age. He wore old and baggy jeans and a pair of scuffed work boots. The black boats, made of rubber on the outside with a removable cloth-like material on the inside, were large and clunky. He approached the two young

TREASURE HUNT 2000

women. Behind him followed his two daughters, ages seven and nine. His children also wore parkas but theirs were relatively new and unstained. "Hi, can I help you find something?" he said pulling his hood back and revealing his face. In one hand he carried a large paper bag and in the other a shovel. He was a large fellow with receding brown hair, and big oval eyes that seemed to smile. "Yeah," said Marci, "do you know where the information office is?" The forty something year old man flashed the teenagers a smile. "Yes, I do," he said. Then changing the subject, he asked. "Are you women out hunting for the medallion?" "Yes!" replied the teens. His daughters began giggling and grinning, "So are we!" they said excitedly in an attempt to find something in common with the older girls. Their father spoke again, "yeah, we go treasure hunting every year. I've personally gone for nearly 35 years." Then he explained that his father had taken him treasure hunting every year from the time he was 10 until the day his oldest daughter Harmony was born. "Have you ever found it?" asked Inga. He laughed. "Nope! Never found it. Come close a bunch of times but never found it. Is this your first time looking for it?" he questioned. "How did you know," replied Inga in a heavy German accent. "No tools of the trade," he said lifting up his shovel to show the young women. His youngest daughter, Melody, more concerned with Inga's accent than her lack of preparation, asked, "where are you from?" "Germany," replied Inga. "Germany!" repeated the little girl. "I'm German too." It was a statement that Inga had heard many times while traveling the United States, Americans claiming to be German. Inga paused, not sure how to respond. In the respite Melody's father corrected, "What she's trying to say is that some of our ancestors are from Germany and we have some relatives that still live over there." Inga smiled at the little girl to keep her from feeling embarrassed.

Her father continued, "The office is over that hill," he said pointing in the direction of a mound of snow. "We'd like to stay and talk longer but we're on our way to lunch," he said while motioning to the large and well used paper bag he held in his hand. With that the father and his daughters departed. Although the building was nowhere to be seen, the cousins took his word for it and climbed the snowy hill. When they reached the summit they could see the building. The building was made of gray bricks and was located at the base of the hill. From a distance the long stone structure

Treasure Hunt 2000

reminded Inga of her school back in Germany. It had double metal doors and small windows, all along the sides. Inside the school, a long hallway provided quick and central access to any class. In case of emergencies the passage also provided for easy departure. The hallway conveniently separated the school along with its classrooms into two equal halves. But what the faculty used for safety and convenience, the students would occasionally use for fun. Sometimes when the teachers were not around, a few of the students would line up at one end and race to the other. At the end of the race they would quickly duck out of sight before the adults appeared.

Continuing on, the young women approached the front door. Inga pulled one of the double doors open and entered first. Marci accompanied close behind. Inside, the building looked nothing like what Inga had expected. Instead of a warm, inviting school environment, this building was designed without expression. To save on money, numerous cubicles filled the room. It was like a big maze. One of the cubicles near the front entrance had a sign on it that read, "Information." Marci and Inga approached and spoke to the attendant. "Hi," said Marci. Her salutation prompted the fellow behind the cubical to rise to his feet. "Hi," he responded while forcing a smile. The fellow, a twenty-six year old park employee, with long hair and a goatee, had been inundated by treasure hunters seeking direction all day long. Although he had a pretty good idea what the girls were looking for, as a matter of formality he asked anyway, "can I help you?" Marci responded, "Do you have any new construction over here?" He nodded his head then handed the two girls a map of the park. On the map he had circled two locations in red. "These," he said, "are the only new construction sights in the entire park." The young women took the map and thanked him kindly. Of the two locations he had circled, one was the construction of a new parking lot. The other was an addition onto an existing library. Because the library seemed the most likely location the teens decided it was best to forgo the parking lot and search only around the library.

Exiting the building, Marci and Inga followed a narrow footpath that led to the library. The library was set high on top of a snowy hill roughly a block and a half from the office. Like most libraries in Minnesota, the Sun Ray Library was made of red brick. Originally built during the 1930's, the

Treasure Hunt 2000

old building had survived fires, tornadoes and even a spree of vandalism during the seventies. Despite its hardships, the library has stood for nearly seventy years and for the most part was in relatively good condition. Its bucolic setting was a popular place for weddings, and lovers. From a distance Inga and Marci saw only a few people standing at the summit near the library. "Good!" said Marci. "There aren't many people, we'll be one of the first." Excited by the prospects of finding the medallion, the young women quickened their pace. It was a steep and slippery climb. In order to get to the summit faster, the young women diverged from the indirect route of the footpath. They preferred instead to climb a direct route up the side of the hill through six inches of virgin snow. As they climbed, often bits of snow would find their way into their shoes and socks. "My feet are getting wet," complained Inga. "Mine too," said Marci, "but we can't stop now, we're almost there." When they came to the summit, the teen's hopes of searching among a small number of people were destroyed. On the other side of the snow ridge the cousins looked down on roughly seven hundred persons, all actively searching for the hidden treasure. Some were digging up mounds of snow with shovels; others clawed at the snow with their hands.

Marci and Inga even saw one man with a large pie pan. Scooping snow into his pan he shook and jiggled the white flakes like a miner panning for gold. The miner wore all black and had a mean disposition. If ever someone would search within three feet of where he was "panning" he would yell and complain. "This is my spot," he shouted at one ten-year-old girl who had no intention of searching but was merely passing by. The frightened girl quickly ran to her parents. Her father later came searching for the fellow. His daughter had given him a description of, "a man with dark clothes and baggy eyes." But because of the large crowd, her father was unable to find him. To Inga and Marci, the hunt for the medallion was like solving a puzzle, something to do for fun. But to the majority, the search for the treasure was a serious business. The treasure hunt was an annual event, which many Minnesotans have looked forward to with great expectation. And with ten thousand dollars, twice as much money as usual at stake, many of the hunters seemed agitated and paranoid. The lure of money took away all their joy, and clouded their judgement. Pushing and shoving for the best locations in which to dig, they behaved like

Treasure Hunt 2000

a pack of dogs scrounging after a single bone. Inga saw a vapid expression on the face of one fellow who had dug a hole roughly four feet in diameter. Refusing to admit his mistake, after digging up all the snow, he continued until he dug up roughly three inches of topsoil. He stood in the base of the pit with his mouth open breathing out large clouds of breath. Both young women shook their heads in disbelief.

Despite their rude awakening as to the seriousness some people placed on the game, the teens began their search. Because they didn't have shovels, they relied entirely on eyesight. Almost immediately, Inga spotted something in the snow out of the corner of her eye. It was round and shiny. As she approached to take a closer look the fellow with the pie pan who had also noticed the object ran and grabbed the object before her. With his hopes high he lifted it out of the snow. When he realized that all he held was an empty soda can he tossed it back into the snow with a scowl. Although his actions were rude it didn't bother Inga. After all it was only a can, and both Inga and Marci saw plenty of other things that needed to be inspected. So they spent the afternoon walking through the park picking up anything that seemed out of the ordinary. After spending almost two hours

TREASURE HUNT 2000

gleaning through hundreds of discarded bottles, cans, pieces of plastic, and newspapers, they decided to "call it quits." "Lets just go home," said Marci. "Tomorrow's clues should give us a better Idea. Who knows, Maybe we're not even in the right park." At that the young women headed home.

Treasure Hunt 2000

Chapter 7

Inga and Marci were gone for roughly four hours. In their absence, Craig took full advantage. Realizing they wouldn't return for hours, Craig seized the opportunity to go see the extreme sports film that the young women had summarily rejected. The documentary was shot on the streets of New York and focused in large part on the 1997 World Skateboard Championships. Craig, a skateboarder himself, just loved watching other ground surfers perform difficult skills. Some skaters could even launch themselves as high as twelve feet off the ground, a process which skaters fondly referred to as "grabbing air." Then they would land ever so gently onto their boards like birds alighting onto a branch. However, the more difficult the skill the more chances there were for mistakes. Even minor misjudgments in timing could

TREASURE HUNT 2000

send skaters flailing to the ground like hapless ducks during hunting season. This process was described by Craig and his skating buddies as "gettin' crunched." It wasn't a very popular film. That is to say, the movie catered predominately to a small minority of extreme sports enthusiasts. But to Craig it was the best movie in town. The film lasted nearly three hours. When it finally ended, Craig, who by now figured his sister and cousin would be on their way back to his apartment, left the theater as quickly as possible and headed straight home. He arrived at the apartment just in time, five minutes ahead of his guests.

While in the middle of changing clothes and getting things ready for dinner, Craig heard two hard raps, knocking at his door. "Coming!" said Craig. After taking a few moments longer, Craig opened the door. His sister and cousin stood in the hall waiting, cold and wet. As they enter, their tennis shoes made the familiar dull squishy sounds that denoted extreme saturation. From the expression on their faces, Craig could see that his cousin and sister didn't have much fun treasure hunting. Both looked awfully tired. Marci and Inga crossed the apartment and took seats on the futon. After a moment or two of fiddling with wet shoelaces, each girl removed their shoes and socks and placed them on top of a nearby radiator to dry. "How was it?" asked Craig as he watched the girls return to the futon and wrap themselves in his blankets. "Cold!" said Marci. "Wet!" responded Inga. Marci continued, "how about you? What did you do today?" Craig paused for a moment. His sister and cousin seemed to lean forward in their seats waiting in anticipation for his response. Should he tell them the truth? Should he say that while they endured arduous labor and cold temperatures he spent the afternoon relaxing in a movie theater eating warm buttered popcorn and sipping chilled bubbly beverages? It was a great temptation. As a kid Craig always enjoyed getting the upper hand on his sister, and now he had a prime opportunity to boast about how much fun he had. A slight smile came to his lips as he considered his options. From the corner of his eye he could see his sister's big brown eyes staring, waiting, for his response. "Nothing much," he said. "I just sat around." His statement though not entirely true put the young women at ease. "Mop you should have seen it," said Marci with what seemed a hint of sorrow in her voice. "We thought we were the only ones who had figured the clues out but when we went to the library it was

TREASURE HUNT 2000

like a mad house. Thousands of people were there." Inga picked up were Marci left off, "And they all brought shovels. We were like a fish out of water." At that both Marci and Inga recounted their entire journey from first to last, sharing both joys and disappointments. From the description they had given him, searching for the medallion appeared a tough and thankless job. And the girls were paying the price.

Occasionally one young woman would cover her mouth then sneeze. Walking around for such a long time in wet shoes had given them slight colds. "Rat!" said Craig. "How you doin', are you alright?" "It's just a sneeze," said Marci while adjusting her blankets to better keep out the cold. "If you dusted your place one in a while, I wouldn't have to sneeze so much." Craig knew Marci was just trying to be tough. Her room back in Rhode Island typically collects much more dust than his apartment. She just didn't want to admit that she might be sick. Concerned that the girls might come down with some horrible sickness, Craig walked over to Marci and placed the palm of his hand on her forehead then compared her temperature with his own. There was no noticeable difference. He repeated the procedure with Inga. The results were the same. Although the girls didn't appear to have a temperature, Craig was still concerned. "Why don't you guys take tomorrow off? You look like you might be coming down with a cold or something," he encouraged. Like a comic who tells a bad joke, at the conclusion of his suggestion, he was greeted with blank stares. Then Marci furrowed her eyebrows, "we're not getting sick!" she proclaimed, surprised that her brother would even suggest that they stop searching. Inga added after a sneeze, "… And even if we are sick, it's no big problem… we've been sick before." Craig's suggestion that the girls rest and relax for a day went over like a lead zeppelin. Despite the fact that searching for the medallion was a tough and arduous job. It was still the best game in town. Why? Because it was challenging and fun! On top of that, the two cousins were best friends, and like best friends they loved working together. Win or lose they would succeed or fail together. Craig took note of their commitment and nodded his head in agreement, "that's cool," he said. "I don't mind if you guys …ah girls go treasure hunting. I just don't want you walking around out there with wet shoes. Mom and dad would be really upset if either of you got meagerly sick. So can you do me a favor and try to keep your feet dry." It was a fair com-

Treasure Hunt 2000

promise, and both parties agreed that if either Marci or Inga began running a temperature they would confine themselves to Craig's apartment and stop hunting for the medallion.

With the agreement the girls turned their attention to more important matters. "Ahh... Craig, are uh ...we eating diner soon?" asked Marci. In their zeal for the medallion, both Inga and Marci had forgotten to eat lunch and so both were hungry. "Yeah," said Craig. "Good idea I'll go make it." Craig headed to the kitchen and began preparing the meal. Marci and Inga waited in the living room. The sizzling sound of meat, as it cooked denoted a welcome departure from yesterday's meal of meatless spaghetti. As dinner fizzled and popped, Inga and Marci turned to one another with big smiles. "He's really making dinner," Inga jokingly whispered to Marci. "What do you think he's making," she added. "I don't know?" said Marci; " it sounds like a big steak." The young women laughed. "Are you making us steak?" Inga yelled to Craig over the sound of searing meat. "Kinda," replied Craig. Then cautioning, "It's a surprise, so don't come in. It's almost done." When he finished cooking he served the meal on paper plates. What he had prepared was a pleasant surprise to both women. After all, everyone likes cheeseburgers. He served each of them one large burger made with one half of a pound of ground beef, two slices of tomato, and topped with a stringy mess of cooked onions. And to spice it up a little, he added two slices of hot pepper cheese. It was a hamburger lover's dream. Having missed lunch, the two girls ate the burgers with relish. Although they ate as much as they could, the women were unable to finish. The sandwiches were just too big. "That was really good," said Inga as she pushed herself away from a half-eaten sandwich. "I didn't know you could cook." Marci, who also could not finish, took a few more nibbles then added jokingly, "yeah, Mop, where did you learn to cook?" Craig responded with his usual coolness, "it's a guy thing," he said. "All men know how to cook hamburgers, it's a prerequisite." The young women laughed while Craig sat with a smug look on his face. "It's an ancient male secret," Craig added, "...passed down from father to father. Don't laugh! Burger-making is serious business among us males," he joked. His warnings went unheeded. Marci and Inga laughed themselves to tears.

After a little more joking around, the girls took showers, changed clothes, and prepared for bed. Why did they

TREASURE HUNT 2000

prepare for bed so early? After dinner, there was nothing in Craig's apartment of interest. If Craig had a TV. they would have gladly stayed up watching movies until late in the morning. Back in Rhode Island, watching late movies and eating salted nuts, was one of their favorite things to do. But with Craig, such luxuries were lacking. With all the preparations complete, Inga and Marci bided Craig a good night and went into the bedroom. Of course they weren't tired, seven thirty was too early for teenage girls to sleep. Instead, they moved the bed near the window and sat watching the stars twinkling in the black of night. "I hope you're not too bummed out," said Marci, "that things didn't quite go as planned." "No, not really," responded Inga, "are you?" "I was at first," said Marci. "But not anymore, I mean finding the medallion would be nice, but it's not like we need the money." "Right," said Inga, "we should keep that in mind we're only searching for fun, not because we have to." Marci nodded her head, "yeah, the moment it stops being fun, we stop searching." Inga also nodded in the affirmative, then looked up into the sky and pointed to a large bright star. "Look at that," she said. "Isn't it beautiful?" Marci looked high overhead and saw the bright vibrant sun of a distant galaxy twinkling. "It's wonderful," she said. Then she added, "wouldn't it be great to travel to distant planets? Then I could easily do a quadruple full. I'd be weightless. But seriously, let's say that a miracle happens and we end up finding the medallion. If you could do anything you wanted with the money what would you do?" Inga thought for a while then responded, "ah... I don't know, maybe... ah... oh I don't know. How about you?" Marci hemmed and hawed as she tried to summarize what she wanted to do with the money. "Uh... I don't know. I guess I just wanna be someone who would use it to change the world for the better." Inga, chuckled adding, "you and me both." The young women sat on the bed stargazing and sharing for quite awhile. Still facing the window, they finally fell asleep leaning against one another, shoulder to shoulder, head to head. Craig checked in on Inga and Marci at around two in the morning. He found them balanced against one another in a deep sleep. Carefully putting each to bed, he pulled the blankets up over their shoulders and tucked them in. The evening passed and before long, morning came.

Treasure Hunt 2000

Treasure Hunt 2000

Chapter 8

With their bed next to the window, the girls were awakened, by the light of the sun. Eager to start the day, they decided to get dressed. Marci, of course, chose a more indirect route to starting the day. Since she wanted to prepare herself for the great challenges of the treasure hunt, Marci decided to make a little challenge of her own. From the bed, she managed to put her hands onto the floor and kick up into a handstand. At this point, her hands were now her feet. Marci practically had four feet because she walked on her hands almost as well as her feet. Now comes the more difficult part. Carefully palming her way to her clothes, Marci thought of an ingenious way to bring them to the bed. When she reached her pile of clothing picked out for the day, she slowly piked down and grabbed her stuff with her feet while

Treasure Hunt 2000

still balancing on her hands. All Marci had to do now was to straighten her body back out and stroll over to the bed. As she did, she let herself down with a plop onto the bed just long enough to put on her clothes and then returned immediately to the handstand. Marci, while still inverted, then headed out of the bedroom, towards the futon, for the final stretch. With the futon in sight, Marci did a snap down to both feet and ran towards her destination. Inches before the futon, she punched off her feet and flipped forward. Having precise "air sense," Marci purposely planned to land safely and totally flat on her back. After she secured her landing Marci quickly rolled over to her stomach, propped up her hands to rest her chin, and smiled while saying, "I'm ready now." Inga and Craig then roared with cheers and laughter. When all three had calmed down from this jolting start of the morning, Inga joined Marci on the futon and listened to Craig read the days' clues from the morning paper. "Minutes tick away and days do pass, the medallion is still hidden, it awaits you at last. Near water and ice your reward doth rest, more up than down so give your back a rest. Come! Do not delay, the reward is true, on a bed of snow it awaits for you. Come by land or by sea, it matters not to us, only that you come leave the rest to us. My speech has ended, I leave you with this, a light in the night makes all things bright."

Craig finished reading, and for a moment everyone was silent. After a minute or two of quietly pondering the meaning of the clues, Craig spoke. "Let's make a list of the most important clues," he said. "I think we have enough information to at least find the right park." Craig got a pen and a piece of paper from the kitchen. Before writing he discussed with the girls which clues were the most important. They settled on six statements.

The first statement, "on public ground the prize is set," was interpreted as having two meanings; first it was confirmation that the medallion was in one of the parks, and second it hinted at the medallion being on the ground, as opposed to hanging in a tree. The second statement, "The discovery could be near, even under your toe," was further confirmation that the prize was located somewhere on the ground. The third statement, "beauty is sweet but passes away," they guessed to be a reference to a park having seasonal plants, probably flowers. The fourth clue, "within the ancient and the new," they be-

TREASURE HUNT 2000

lieved referred to the remodeling or the addition onto an old building. The fifth clue, "come by land or by sea it matters not to us," they were certain was their most important lead. Because it was cold out side, a three or four-inch layer of ice covered nearly every body of water except the Mississippi River. And finally the sixth clue, "a light in the night makes all things bright," they concluded referred to a light in the park that would illuminate where the medallion was hidden. Thus it was understood that hunting for the medallion was best done after 6:30 P.M., for that was when the park lights throughout the entire city were scheduled to turn on.

With a summary of the clues laid out before them, Craig unfolded his map of St. Paul and circled in red all the parks that could be reached by boat as well as land. There were only four parks that fit that description: Hidden Falls Regional Park, Pigs Eye Park, Harriet Island Regional Park, and Baker Valley Park. All four parks could be reached via the Mississippi River. With the list of possible locations reduced to four, Craig telephoned each park to inquire about new construction projects or any notable flowerbeds. His inquiries produced mixed results. All four parks claimed no knowledge of any new construction projects, or renovations. And on the issue of flowers only one, Harriet Island Regional Park, claimed to have a flowerbed, but only during the summer. Although the preliminary results were inconclusive, the youth's interpretation of the clues made Harriet Island Park appear the most likely location for the medallion.

"What do ya think?" asked Craig while pointing to the park with a highlighter. Marci and Inga moved closer to the map to get a better look. Harriet Island Park was located in the northeast corner of St. Paul. It was a large football shaped peninsula which was connected to the city of St. Paul by a singular narrow path of earth about ten feet in width and forty feet in length. From the map, Harriet Island appeared a perfect place for the teenagers to explore. Surrounded on 320 degrees by water the park was quaint and secluded. The two explorers looked at one another and smiled big smiles of excitement. Because one of the clues alluded to the night as the best time for the search, it was agreed that the young women would arrive at around 4:30 in the afternoon and search until 9:00 o'clock in the evening at the latest. This time frame allowed ample opportunity to

Treasure Hunt 2000

discover the location of flower gardens and any obscure construction projects before the sunset. Once the locations were discovered it was assumed that Inga and Marci would station themselves nearby and wait for dark. When the evening lights would come on, they presumably would reveal to the children specific locations in which to search. For Inga and Marci, who were anxious to begin their second day treasure hunting, time seemed to move slowly. To help pass the time, they busied themselves by playing with the walkie-talkies.

Marci initiated the first move, "hey Inga, go into the bedroom so we can test out the walkie-talkies." "OK, but let's have some code names and phrases to use so the other hunters won't follow our leads," replied Inga. As Inga walked into Craig's bedroom, the girls both thought of different things to say. Marci wanted to be funny so she started the conversation, "This is 'Vaulting Horse' calling for… " Before she could think of a name to call her cousin, Inga blurted out, "Bookworm." Trying to keep from laughing, Marci continued the acting. She wanted to create a code to tell Inga she had found the treasure. Finally she came up with one, "OK, 'Bookworm', I have found the restroom." Wanting to be equally creative, Inga coded a phrase that explained what they were to do next. "That's good 'Vaulting Horse', you go ahead and wash up and I'll meet you at home." Marci jokingly added, "neh, I don't think so. I don't want to go home anymore, now that I've found the bathroom I feel like a new woman. You know I got places to go, people to see, and things to do. Tell you what, you go home and I'll see ya when I see ya." At that, both were overcome with giggles. The more they added to the joke the more they laughed. When they finally finished horsing around, they had lunch and waited a few hours longer and had an early dinner. At 3:50 P.M. they left for the Island.

Before departing, since neither of the girls had winter boots, Craig gave each girl two large forty gallon garbage bags along with two rubber bands. "This is to keep your feet dry," he said. "If you have to walk in deep snow, just put one on each foot, and use the rubber band to hold it in place." He demonstrated for the girls how it would look. To Marci and Inga the demonstration looked abhorrent. It was, so the girls thought, the worst fashion faux pas in the history of womankind. Although they were determined never to put the ugly bags on their feet, they pretended he had given them valuable advice. "That's a good idea," said Marci,

Treasure Hunt 2000

"Thanks." Inga, knowing Marci couldn't possibly be serious, just looked at Craig with a slight Mona Lisa type smile that belied the truth and nodded her head. When the time came, Craig walked them to the bus stop. The bus arrived at 4:12 P.M. The young women boarded and Craig returned to his apartment.

Treasure Hunt 2000

Treasure Hunt 2000

Chapter 9

The bus traveled down Grand. It stopped frequently to let new passengers on and old passengers off. After twenty minutes of stopping and starting, it reached its destination. At the corner of Lexington and Sibley the driver stopped the bus to let the children off. Marci looked out the window at the river below. She expected to see a mass of land rising out of the water, but there was nothing. "Where is Harriet Island?" Marci asked. "Oh that, " said the driver. "That's about four blocks up," he said pointing to the right. "Just follow the river, you can't miss it." The children stepped off into the snow. The doors closed, then the bus rumbled down the road into the distance until it faded out of sight. It was a pleasant winter day. The temperature was mild and the wind calm. With their coat pockets loaded with rubber bands, plastic bags, and walkie-talkies, the young women did as they were directed and followed the Mississippi. The river, the fourth largest in the world, meandered its way from Itasca State Park all the way down to the Gulf of Mexico. In times past, it was considered one of the most important resources in all of Minnesota. Businesses and cities sprouted up all along its banks seeking to utilize the power of rushing water to generate electricity or transport goods from the north to the south.

They continued walking. After climbing a sharp incline, the river widened and turned to the left. At the apex of the incline, no longer hidden by the horizon or the topography, they looked into the dark bluish gray Mississippi water and saw Harriet Island. From Inga and Marci's perspective, the enclave, which was covered with a dense layer of snow, looked more like an iceberg with trees than an isle. "Is that it?" questioned Inga. "I think so," replied Marci. "It doesn't look like much of a park," added her cousin. Marci nodded her head in agreement. "No it doesn't," she said. Despite the bleak appearance of the park, the two continued walking along the Mississippi. When they found the path that connected Harriet Island with the mainland, they crossed over. It was shaped like and egg and situated in the center of the Mississippi. On one side, near the edge of the Island, was a large hill. When approached from the left the hill prevented some from seeing its true beauty. Unlike most parks which brag about their amenities, Harriet Island had very few. There were no tennis courts, and no ice skating rinks. The only notable amenities were peace and solitude. During the summer, people often came to lie on its green grass and unwind. Inga, who enjoyed quaint and quiet places, turned to Marci, "this is a great place," she said. The girls continued walking. On their right they noticed a small square building made of wood. "There's the information office," said Marci. Changing their course, the two headed for the office.

The small one room building was nothing special. Inside were only the barest of necessities, one desk, one chair, and one male attendant. Both Marci and Inga spoke with the park employee at length. He was friendly and quite helpful. "There are two flower gardens," he told them. "Although you can't see them now, when summer comes again there will be one on either side of the building." He continued, "and as far as new construction projects, the only one that I

Treasure Hunt 2000

know of is the sidewalk replacement that's going on near that tree over there." With his hand he directed the girls to a big tree with large spindly branches. The tree was about three hundred feet to the right of the building. Before departing the two young women thanked him for his kindness. "No problem," he said. "It was my pleasure."

Exiting the building, the young women decided that they should separate. Marci would search the flowerbeds and Inga would search the sidewalk construction sight. As they separated, occasionally they would check the range of their walkie-talkies. "Testing… one… two… three, Inga can you hear me?" "I can hear you but there's static," Inga shouted back. By the time each arrived at their respective destinations, the static was so bad they had to shout in order to be heard. As the park slowly began to fill, the cousins realized that they were not the only ones to suspect Harriet Island as the hiding place. By 5:45 P.M. the park was packed with people from all walks of life. Inside the flower garden, large numbers of people searched for the medallion. Because of the crowd, there was a lot of pushing and shoving. With intense frowns and scowls, hunter vied against hunter for the best places to dig. Marci, who stood in the center of the mob, observed their angry expressions and frenzied activities in amazement. Not a single smile was seen or laugh was heard only frowns and grunts. While she watched all the activity, a fellow who dug behind her carelessly lifted his shovel and wielded it into the air. His shovel would have hit Marci in the back, if not for the kindness of a stranger who raised his hand to block the blow. "Hey! Girl," he shouted. Marci turned around to see a hooded figure in a green coat. Two children stood by his side. The gymnast recognized the two children as Harmony and Melody. "Hi," said Marci. "Hi," answered the two sisters. "How are you doing?" ask the younger girl. Marci laughed, "fine, how about you?" "I'm fine," said the little girl. Just then her father interrupted their discussion. "What are you doing out here by yourself?" he asked with concern. "I'm not," she replied. "I'm here with my cousin Inga." After a brief pause, she pointed to a crowd of people a few hundred feet away. The father turned to see where Marci was pointing. He saw in the distance a bustling mob of people with shovels and pick axes shoveling snow and hacking at ice. "You shouldn't separate. You girls..."

As he was speaking the thing which Marci and Inga

Treasure Hunt 2000

had been waiting for finally, arrived. The sun slowly set and the park night-lights turned on. Distracted by the lights, Marci no longer paid attention to the conversation. "I have to go," she said. Without waiting for a response, Marci departed. Pushing her way through the fervent crowd of diggers. She headed for the nearest park light. Once there, she searched around the fixture but found nothing. She repeated the process with five other nearby lamps and had the same results. After searching for a while, she began to think that maybe the treasure was somewhere by Inga. With the aid of her walkie-talkie, she gave Inga a call. "Inga… Inga," she shouted into the receiver. "Can you hear me?" There was a long pause. And then Inga responded, "yeah… I can hear you," she yelled in response. Because of her location Inga's voice was not clear. It was mingled with static and the clamoring of strangers in the background. "How's it going over there? Did you find the bathroom?" she spoke in code. "No," replied Inga. "I'm still looking. The people over here are pretty mean so it's hard to find anything." In the back ground while Inga spoke. Marci heard two fellows arguing with one another, "get off my foot!" shouted the first. "Look!" said the other, "I was… here first, if you have a problem with your foot occasionally gettin stepped on go find your own place to dig." Inga spoke again, "see what I mean." There was a long pause. Marci was distracted. "Marci, can you hear me?" Inga shouted into the receiver. Still only partially paying attention, this time Marci managed to pull herself together just long enough to mutter a single word, "wow!" Although Marci's utterance was indistinct, Inga knew that she had discovered something important. "What is it?" she yelled to get her full attention. "Within the ancient and the new," said Marci forgetting to speak in code. "It doesn't refer to an addition onto an existing building," she yelled with a note of laughter in her voice. "Look at that big mound of snow over to the left and tell me what you see." Inga turned to her left and saw the large hill of snow that Marci referred to. Protruding from the side she saw for the first time the ice castle. The castle was set into the side of the mountain of snow. During the day and from a distance, it looked inconspicuous. But during the evening, when the park-lights turned on, it was illuminated from inside. The walls of the castle looked a soft bluish-yellow. "I didn't know that was there," said Inga, "but do you really think they would put the medallion over there?" "I think so," said Marci, Because

Treasure Hunt 2000

castles are old, but the construction, is new and before the lights came on we didn't recognize it." Inga following the same vain added, "and it looks beautiful and because it's ice it passes away, you're right," said Inga, "I'll meet you there." With walkie-talkies in hand, Inga and Marci headed to the castle of ice. In order not to attract attention, they made their approach as inconspicuous as possible. Both teens could see that the castle looked empty. And both wanted to avoid, if possible, all the pushing and shoving they had previously experienced.

# Treasure Hunt 2000

Treasure Hunt 2000

Treasure Hunt 2000

Chapter 10

Since Inga was closer to the castle it was expected that she would arrive first. "When you get there," said Marci. "Check around the lights." "Of course," replied Inga. Marci watched her cousin as she began the journey. Separating from the crowd, she waded through the snow. As she continued watching, she noticed something that seemed rather odd. Behind Inga, another figure had also decided to leave the crowd. Because of the high snow, the figure followed the exact same footsteps as her cousin. Marci called to Inga on her walkie-talkie. "Inga, how are you doing?" "Fine," said her cousin. "OK, I have something to tell you. I want you to keep walking and don't get frightened." Her words were a little unsettling. Usually telling someone not to get frightened implies that they had a good reason to be frightened.

Treasure Hunt 2000

"What is it?" asked Inga. "Remember don't get frightened," her cousin repeated. "Now don't turn around, but I think there's someone following you." The news that she was being stalked caught Inga totally off guard. Marci saw her cousin instantly tense up and began to walk faster. "What are you doing Inga," said Marci. "Stop walking so fast, I can see him, he's not close to you." Hearing that he wasn't as close as she had thought, Inga relaxed and slowed her pace. "How close is he?" she asked. "About a hundred feet," answered Marci. "What do you want to do? Do you have a plan?" asked Inga. Marci, figuring the fellow had overheard their conversation and thus had a pretty good idea where the medallion was hidden responded, "yeah he's like about a minute behind so when you get to the castle look for the medallion as fast as you can. If you can find it before he comes, hide it somewhere else and when I get there we'll both go retrieve it." Inga agreed with the plan and continued to pretend that she was unaware she was being followed.

It took her only a matter of a few minutes to reach the ice castle. For support purposes the castle was built into the side of a large mound of snow. The mound, which supported the castle, stood nearly twenty-four stories high. The ice castle, which was not as tall, stood roughly twenty stories in height. In celebration of the start of a new millennium, the city of St. Paul had pulled out all the stops. The ice castle that ushered in the millennium was a full two hundred and forty feet high. It was a large sprawling complex with over thirty spires of varying heights jutting up out of the mountain, like needles out of a pin cushion. The entire structure was built utilizing over twenty-five million pounds of snow and ice. Stacked one on top of another, the ice that made up the walls looked to Inga like large translucent blue bricks. The complex was divided into three main sections. Although the majority of the structure was composed of solid ice one section was not. And because it was not solid it was the only section that allowed visitors to come and experience life from the inside. If one desired to enter, they merely had to pass under a single Gothic arch, ten feet high and four feet wide. The entrance was guarded on either side by iced statues of twin male lions, with mouths agape and teeth showing. Inga, who had seen many castles in Germany, but never one made of ice, was amazed at the attention to detail. Although she would have loved to explore the castle in depth, there was no time. Because the fellow who followed her was close behind, she was forced to limit her exploration to the most likely location for the medallion. There was only one section of the massive structure that seemed inviting. The rest was surrounded by a wall of ice that cautioned sight seers to stay away. Hurrying pass the big cats, Inga entered the castle.

On the inside, the castle looked to Inga like a mansion made of crystal. There were chairs, tables, and a fire place with logs all meticulously crafted out of ice. It was a spectacular sight. The vaulted forty foot tall A-framed ceiling was a thing of beauty to behold. Three lights placed in strategic locations inside this section of the castle made the cold ice appear warm and inviting. From the outside it appeared to glow in the night. Overhead, suspended by rope from the vaulted ceiling hung two chandeliers. The chandeliers dangled nearly twenty feet in the air. For added safety an, iron cross bar inside each chandelier was used for added stability. The two large chandeliers resembling massive glass wind chimes hung on both sides of a large beam of ice. The beam, poised nearly eleven feet above Inga's head, was forty feet long, two feet wide, and two feet high. Used as structural support, the beam connected the front of the building

TREASURE HUNT 2000

with the back. The thought of having thousands of pounds of ice looming over her head gave Inga mixed feelings of awe and fear. Suppressing her desire to "bolt," Inga hurriedly searched around the base of the indoor spotlights, but found nothing. She was about to "call it quits" when she noticed a light ray, reflecting off the ceiling, illuminated a small section of the floor. The floor was covered with about two inches of snow. Quickly running her fingers through the illuminated sections of snow, Inga located a small circular object. She brought it to the surface. The flimsy object, about the size of a coaster, was a translucent-yellow color. Her first impression of the disk was that it was a peace of a child's toy that had broken off and been discarded. It was in actuality what she was searching for. It was the medallion. With little regard, Inga brushed the disk aside and threw it high into the air. The discarded plastic flipped through the air and landed overhead on top of the beam. Her actions were not unusual. Over the years, the inconspicuous look of the medallion had prompted many to mistake its value. Last year one fellow, while cleaning, even mistook it for a peace of trash. He threw it into the garbage. It was later found by an overjoyed sanitation worker that subsequently turned it

Treasure Hunt 2000

in and claimed his reward.

Outside, Inga heard the crunching sound of snow and ice as the stranger who had followed her made his way up the steps. In a matter of a few seconds he was inside the room. "Hi," he said in an inviting and formal voice, like that of a salesman. Inga turned and saw for the first time who had been following her. A large fellow, dressed immaculately in a black wool overcoat, dark gray pants and white shirt, loomed by the entrance. He stood six feet six inches in height and weighed about 250 pounds. His hair was entirely gray and well groomed. Large dark circles surrounding his green eyes gave the impression that he had been awake for a long time. "Hi," Inga responded nervously. "Hey! What are you doing? Are you searching for the medallion?" he asked Inga in an inquisitive and friendly tone. Suspecting that he already knew what she was doing inside the castle, Inga answered him truthfully. "Yes," she said. He continued, "did you find anything?" "No, I thought I did but it was just a peace of a kid's toy." When she mentioned finding the kid's toy, Inga noticed a sarcastic smile slowly forming on the man's thin lips. "Oh, that's nice," he said, pretending to be interested. "I like toys, I found one just yesterday. What kind of toy did you find?" he asked. "I don't know it looked like some kind of coaster," she said. "A coaster?" he asked. "What color was it?" His questioning had now become disturbingly odd. Why would an adult be interested in kids' toys, she wondered. "It was yellow," she replied. When she mentioned the color, the man appeared both anxious and agitated. The dramatic change in his disposition spoke volumes. It was at that moment Inga realized that the small plastic object she had thrown aside was more than likely the medallion. The man continued, "oh that sounds nice. Where did you put it?" In order not to raise the man's suspicion, Inga quickly pointed to the far end of the castle. "I threw it over there," she said. After giving the girl a suspicious glance, the fellow hurried over to where Inga had directed.

While he searched the far corner of the building, Marci arrived. Inga who had contemplated making a run for it breathed a sigh of relief. Taking note of the stranger's location, Marci headed straight to Inga and whispered in soft airy tones. "What's going on?" Inga, who was happy to see her, smiled a big smile and whispered. "I think I've found it." "You did? Where is it?" asked Marci. Inga glanced at the beam that hung over her head. "Up there," she said. All their whispering caught the attention of the fellow searching in back. He rose to his full height and approached the girls. "Well I haven't found it yet," he said interrupting their transference of secrets. "But that's alright," he warned, "I'll search this place all night if I have to," he said with his arms folded. His statement was a veiled threat. By now he figured that Inga had discovered the general location of the medallion. No doubt she was probably waiting for him to leave so she could begin digging. The girls, seeing that he was unwilling to leave, discussed their options. After a few minutes of whispering, they settled on a plan.

In preparation for getting the medallion, Inga and Marci took three of the four forty-gallon plastic bags Craig had given them to keep their feet dry. They decided to rip them open, so that they formed long sheets of plastic. Then they tied the sheets together end to end, forming a long rope. On one end of the rope, Marci tied into the plastic some pieces of ice weighing roughly two pounds. Unaware as to what the girls were trying to accomplish, the fellow with the dark circles around his eyes could only watch and wait. And he wouldn't have to wait long. Once the rope was finished Marci took it and headed to the far end of the castle.

She wanted to put as much distance between herself and the stranger as possible. Inga headed in the opposite direction and waited near the arch. Between them, stood the stranger. His face was now in a scowl. In order to keep track of each child, his eyes were in a constant state of movement shifting from one to the other. Marci waited for the right time. When she saw his eyes shift towards Inga, she made her move. Like a cowgirl preparing to lasso a calf, she twirled the plastic rope in the air and threw the weighted-end over her head in the direction of the beam. With the rope wrapped around the beam she began climbing. As she climbed, the rope slowly loosened its grip while rocking to and fro. Finally, with Marci five feet off the ground, the rope gave out completely. Marci flailed and crashed hard onto the frozen ground below. The stranger, who had seen her clumsy fall, laughed and laughed. His boisterous laughter echoed from wall to wall. "Is that where it is?" he bellowed while still laughing. "Is it up there?" Marci was silent. With her left hand she motioned to Inga that she was all right and to stay by the arch. As she rose from the floor, her black jacket had become covered with so much snow it appeared gray.

Because her second option for mounting the beam re-

Treasure Hunt 2000

quired freedom of movement, Marci took her jacket off and threw it on the floor. She then turned to face the still laughing stranger. "What are you going to do now, beat me up?" he chortled while holding his belly. Marci furrowed her brow and walked towards him, counting her paces as she went. At twenty-five paces she turned again and ran back in the opposite direction. Ten paces from the wall she increased her speed. Finally she leaped onto the wall and continued running. Her feet dug into the cracks were brick met brick. Her momentum, along with her skill as a gymnast, allowed her to run nearly ten feet straight up. When she reached the beam, she grabbed hold with both legs and both arms. It was an amazing feat that made all that watched silent. Marci, who still clung onto the beam hanging upside down, twisted and pulled until she straddled on top like she would on a balance beam. Then she looked at Inga and smiled. "I made it," she said. Inga, who had held her breath, breathed out a sigh. Then, following their plan, she nodded her head and quickly left the building.

Marci was now alone with the tall man. "How did you get up there," he said while trying to climb the same wall Marci had run up. His efforts to climb the wall were futile. From above Marci watched his comical attempt with amusement. "What? Do you think the medallion is up here?" She said imitating his speech patterns and laughter. The thought of being teased by a girl infuriated him. He ran towards Marci and jumped at her feet. If not for her quick reflexes he would have grabbed them. But with cat like agility, Marci sprang to her feet. Crouched on the beam she watched his many frantic leaps in amusement. "Come on," she said, "you can do better than that. A big boy like you ought to be able to get up here with no problem." After a little more teasing, Marci carefully stood up. Although the beam was wider than what she was used to in gymnastics, she found walking across it to be more difficult. This beam was made of ice. Almost every step she made resulted in some amount of sliding. It was a frightening situation stepping onto a slightly melted section of the beam. Her foot slid nearly a foot to the left. It stopped only after nearly half her foot had gone off the edge. While she wobbled on the edge of disaster, the misstep came as encouragement to the fellow who waited below. He attempted to startle the girl by screaming as loud as he could, but the girl remained unstartled. She regained her footing and continued towards

Treasure Hunt 2000

the medallion. The medallion lay twenty feet away, roughly the midpoint of the beam. She approached with caution. Each step brought new challenges. Sometimes the supporting ice was straight and flat like a wooden beam, but unfortunately at other times it was full of slants and curves. Every step she made brought a clamor of yells and screams from below. The pressure was great. Although it was cold inside and Marci wore no jacket, she was sweating.

It was similar to the nervousness she experienced at last year's state meet. Her team was last on the balance beam and she was the last competitor. Marci needed to perform a flawless routine in order for her team to take first place. She knew everyone was depending on her, so the tension was building. Mounting the beam with a front tuck was a risky move, but she performed it without mishap, only a slight bobble. The rest of the routine was sheer poetry, but Marci was still worried. "Good job," said her coach. "Are you sure? What about my mount?" responded Marci nervously. Trying to relieve Marci of her fear, her coach gave some reassuring words. "Oh you covered up really well. Don't worry about it. We have this championship in the bag." Marci used those very words to encourage herself. "We have this medallion in the bag," she whispered under her breath. "Don't worry!"

Marci continued on. "The hard part is over," she said to herself, "just stay calm." In the center of the support she located the medallion. She lifted it from the plank and showed it to the fellow below. "Look!" she said. "I have the medallion. The game is over." The stranger laughed, "Game?" he questioned. "You don't know what you're talking about. This is no game. This is business and in business it's every man for himself. From his jacket, the stranger took out his pie pan and threw it as hard as he could at Marci. Marci instinctively moved to the left, while the pan, flying through the air like a Frisbee, whistled past her ear and hit the wall with a clang. "OK," said Marci. "I'm outta here!" At that Marci leaped from the beam onto one of the chandeliers. Her landing caused some of the delicate bits and pieces to break off and shower the evil man below. Then swinging the chandelier to and fro, she purposely crashed its metal prongs into the wall. Again and again she hit the wall, causing large pieces of ice to break off and fall to the ground. In no time, all her efforts produced a small hole in the wall. While she worked from above, the fellow below would occasionally pick up some of the larger pieces of ice that had broken off and threw them at her. For the most part, his efforts were unsuccessful, except for one large piece that hit her leg, causing her to wince in pain.

When the pain subsided, she continued on. After many strikes the castle had now developed a substantial hole. When what was left of the chandelier swung again to the hole, Marci placed her hands inside the opening and hung on tight to its rough edges. After determining that the ice was strong enough to support her weight, she climbed up and through the hole onto the roof of the castle. Outside, the night air was cold, and to make things even more difficult, the castle roof was slanted. In order to keep from falling off the edge, Marci pressed herself against the cold hard ice and clawed her way to the back of the castle. Since the rear of the castle was set into a large hill of snow, it provided the easiest way to get down without jumping. After creeping along the side of the roof, she finally stepped off onto what appeared a barren mountain of snow. "Inga, are you there?" she whispered into the shadow. Inga stood up from behind a ridge of ice and motioned to Marci to come. Marci hurried over. On the other side of the ridge she saw what Inga had prepared for their escape. Inga's last plastic bag lay on the ground near a steep incline. It was knotted at either end so it looked similar to a canoe. The floor of the canoe-shaped bag was lined with large pieces of discarded cardboard and Inga's jacket. "Where is he?" asked Inga. "Is he still around?" Marci shrugged her shoulders. After she escaped from the castle she lost track of him, "he could be anywhere," she said. Inga climbed into the homemade sled flowed by Marci. "He might be close. Are you ready?" Marci nodded her head.

    Then with a few pushes, they were speeding down the hill. The cold wind as it blew against their faces was almost unbearable. Inga, who sat in front and thereby got the brunt of the wind, would occasionally turn her head to the side to keep the cold air from hitting her directly. They headed in the general direction of a large crowd. Marci kept careful watch from the rear of the sled to see if the evil fellow pursued, but there was no sign of him. Ahead, Inga saw a row of trees. "To the left!" she yelled signaling for Marci to lean with her to the left. She did. The sled gradually turned to the left avoiding the spiny branches of a pine tree by a few feet. As they straightened out, the girls continued their jour-

Treasure Hunt 2000

ney down the slope. Further down, they hit a patch of glazed ice. The ice increased their speed. The faster they traveled the colder they became. Because of the drop in temperature their red ears began to throb in pain. They were now travelling about forty miles per-hour. Trees and bushes seemed to whip by in the blink of an eye. Neither Inga nor Marci had ever sledded so fast, both were frightened and cold. Their rapid speed mixed with the icy surface made steering the sled practically impossible. All they could do was to hope for the best and hold on tight. The sled approached a mound of snow and ice. "Hold on," screamed Inga. The sled traveled up the hill, then launched into the air. The flight was thrilling. The landing was rough. With a crackly scraping sound, the homemade sled came back into contact with snow and ice. The hard landing ripped a large hole into the outer shell and showered the faces of both young women with cold wet snow. As they traveled further, the sled slowly began to disintegrate. After leaving a long trail of plastic and paper, the teens and remnants of the sled came to a halt.

Quickly, springing to their feet, Inga and Marci continued their journey on foot. They ran as fast as they could to a nearby crowd of treasure hunters. While weaving through the crowd of unhappy hunters, the trembling teens, covered with snow, were noticed by Benjamin and his daughters. "What are you doing? Where are your jackets?" he questioned in the form of a demand. "We lost them," said the girls. "No way," he said observing that both young ladies looked in disarray. "Who took your jackets?" No one!" said the girls. At that, Benjamin, a large fellow, took his coat off and wrapped the single jacket around both girls. The green jacket, which he usually wore when working, had a strong smell of earth and grass. "I'm taking you girls home! Where do you live?" Anyone who knew Marci even a little bit knew that she rarely responded favorably to demands. She considered his statement to be an open invitation to ridicule and embarrassment. If not for the presence of Inga, who nudged Marci and whispered, "I'm cold," the father would have been roundly criticized for his lack of tact. Overlooking his fault, Marci informed him that they lived in an apartment on the corner of Snelling and Grand. On route to the car, they weaved through large crowds of people. Backs bent by long hours at the dig, faces smudged by soil and covered with snow, mouths grimaced in arduous labor, the crowd, unaware that the treasure had been found, continued to toil.

Treasure Hunt 2000

"What is there about treasure hunting that make people so unhappy," asked Inga. "It's suppose to be a game," said Benjamin. "But many treat it like it's the most important thing in the world, as if finding the Medallion would solve all their problems."

As they continued walking a little distance away, Inga and Marci saw the well-groomed fellow who had chased them. With his eyes darting back and forth, he looked through the crowd searching for the young women. The closer he approached, the faster their hearts began to beat. In order to avoid his evil eyes, Marci and Inga slowed their pace and maneuvered so as to hide behind Benjamin. Considering that they were well hidden, they were surprised to hear the low hissy voice of the stranger. "Hi, Benjamin," said the stranger as he approached, "What happened to your jacket?" Benjamin stopped, "oh hi Dick, I loaned it to some friends of mine," he said as he moved aside revealing their location. When Dick saw the two young women, his face seemed to grow hard as his muscles tensed and his eyes protruded. Benjamin, noticing the change in his countenance stepped forward in front of the children and asked, "is anything wrong?" Dick trying to hide his anger relaxed his face and forced a smile. "No," he said, "just a little indigestion. I had some really spicy food for supper this evening." Benjamin grunted then nodded his head. "I see," he said. "Well I'd like to stay and talk longer, but we have to be going. Hope you feel better and good luck." As they were leaving, Benjamin noticed an expression of anger slowly returning to Dick's face.

They continued on. After a little more walking, they finally reached Benjamin's old car. His car, a 1985 station wagon, was rusty and dirty, but had plenty of room. Marci and Inga sat comfortably in the back seat while Benjamin, Harmony, and Melody sat up front. After pumping the gas and turning the key five or six times, the car started. The car exited the parking lot and headed out onto the road. "You must have found the medallion," said the father. His statement surprised his daughters. Both turned around to see the teens and their expressions. Both Inga and Marci were shocked at this statement. "Why do you think that?" asked Marci. "I don't know, just a feeling I got when I saw Dick look at you. Everyone knows that Dick would do anything for money and when I saw Dick look at you, it was like he perceived you as a threat. So I put two and two together.

Treasure Hunt 2000

Am I right?" After a long pause, both girls nodded in the affirmative. "Well, he's gone now. You've found it. You should be rejoicing." Said Benjamin noting a somber expression on the face of both girls through his mirror. "Yeah," said Marci. "But we don't need the money, and at the park there were so many people that looked like they needed the money but didn't find it." When she finished her weighty statement, the car drove in relative silence. In the back seat the two cousins whispered to one another. At the corner of Snelling and Grand, the car came to a stop. "You're home," spoke the driver after a long period of silence. He continued, "I was thinking about what you said. It's true, you might not need the money now, but you don't know what the future holds. God does everything for a reason." "You're right," said the cousins as they climbed from the back seat and headed to the apartment. "Thanks for the ride."

Inside the apartment, after changing their clothes, they explained their entire day's journey from first to last. Craig was excited to hear the story. "I wish I could have been there," he said. "Are you gals alright." "Fine!" responded each. Their adventure was over. As expected they stayed in Minnesota for three more days. Since they had lost their coats, Craig bought each a new coat. The respective coats were similar to the styles that the children had lost. "This should keep you warm," he said. "Just try not to lose them." Their adventure at Harriet Island had given both girls a cold. So as agreed upon, they spent the last three days being pampered by Craig and recuperating in his apartment. "I never knew being sick in America was so much fun," said Inga over a bowl of ice cream and hot apple pie. "Shh," said Marci raising her index finger to her lips in a caution of silence, while chewing a mouthful of pie. "It's an ancient girls' secret passed down from mother to daughter," she whispered with a wink. "Don't tell him." The three days passed quickly and before long they were back in Rhode Island.

Benjamin and his daughters returned home at about 9:15 P.M. As his children hurried into the house he reached into the back seat to retrieve the jacket he lent Marci and Inga. Under the coat he found a note. The note read.

> "Thank you, so much for your kindness, sometimes changing the world is as simple as changing the life of one person."

And under the note he found the medallion. He sought to

TREASURE HUNT 2000

return it, but in the end was unable to locate his generous passengers.

Treasure Hunt 2000